The Fungo Society

A QUICK BASEBALL MYSTERY

JEFF STANGER

Blue Trolley Press

Carmel, Indiana

Blue Trolley Press
10550 Breckenridge Drive
Carmel, Indiana 46033
www.bluetrolleypress.com

Publisher's Note: This is a work of fiction. Names, characters, places, and incidents are a product of the author's imagination. Locales and public names are sometimes used for atmospheric purposes. Any resemblance to actual people, living or dead, or to businesses, companies, events, institutions, or locales is completely coincidental.

Edited by: Terry Sowka
Cover Design: Justin Bessler
Book Layout ©2013 BookDesignTemplates.com
Ordering Information:
Quantity sales. Special discounts are available on quantity purchases by corporations, associations, and others. For details, contact the "Special Sales Department" at the address above.

The Fungo Society/ Jeff Stanger. -- 1st ed.
ISBN-13: 978-1-939579-01-0

Other books by this author:
Trolley Dodgers
Kansaska
Facts Cause Cancer

For all the collectors.
– Jeff Stanger

I found his pants.
– Quick

There have been two great Spring Breaks in my life. Both involved baseball, sex, warm weather, and some level of danger. Let me tell you a little about the first. When I was twelve years old, I had to stand up in front of class on a cold wintry day in March and talk about what I did on Spring Break. Growing up relatively poor in Indiana, I didn't get to go on Spring Break like the other kids. So, I made up the following story:

"Last week for Spring Break, my family went to Vero Beach to watch the Dodgers at spring training. My dad is a Dodgers fan, but I love the Reds. They played one game against each other during the week and the Reds won 5-2. I met Tommy Lasorda, got a bat signed by Johnny Bench, and two college girls showed me their breasts. Life will be pretty much be downhill from here." After taking a few moments to compose herself, my teacher sent me to the principal's office.

I wasn't really sure what she was upset about, the made-up story or the breasts. Turns out it was mostly the breasts and at twelve years old, I learned a valuable lesson. Most people get squeamish when you talk about breasts. This is even more perplexing because women go to such great lengths to highlight, enhance, and draw focus to them. Doesn't matter. My advice to you is glance, do not stare, and never discuss. Keep that in mind or society will shun you.

As for the speech, I was able to negotiate a compromise. I got a B+ by agreeing to serve after-school detention and promise to never again reference the body parts that must not be named in public places in the Bible Belt. The B+ came from my pointing out that the speech was supposed to entertain and inform and I had done both with aplomb, if I do say so myself. I learned I had negotiating skills that later would serve me well in my chosen profession: baseball artifacts dealer.

My name is Jonathan Quick and I am the proprietor and founder of Quick Baseball Artifacts. I deal mostly in baseball, as that is my specialty, but I've been known to throw in a football or basketball relic from time to time.

Many of the things I search for are things that wind up in museums—or have been stolen from them. Or, they wind up in the private collections of wealthy baseball fans. These are the things for which people will pay top dollar. And if they don't feel like paying top dollar, they will steal, kill, and occasionally do other depraved things to acquire them. I'm sure you're wondering if I've stolen, killed or done depraved things to get my hands on a piece of baseball history. The answer to that is very complicated. In the strictest sense of the word, yes I have. But you have to understand that it was all in the name of restoring some important artifact to its rightful place: its true owner or a museum. You could say that I'm sort of an "off the books" employee of certain famous sports museums that would prefer my efforts on their behalf remain discreet.

As for the sex, well these things can't be avoided in my line of work. Sometimes the best way to get to the secret basement with the hoard of artifacts is through the bedroom. That is one of many reasons you won't find my name listed as an employee of any reputable museum. I have a slightly depraved approach to curating.

You're probably wondering about that second greatest Spring Break by now. Did it come in college along with some tales of drunken debauchery in Florida or South Padre Island? No. Was it a fishing adventure off the coast of Southern California? No. Did it involve exotic women in some foreign country? Sadly, no. My second greatest Spring Break happened in Phoenix and involved murder, grumpy old men, sports auctions, and various leisurely entanglements with members of the opposite sex. Some of my closest companions (some of whom you will meet very soon) might say that I just described my usual day-to-day existence—minus the grumpy old men. However, it was that group of old retired ballplayers that makes this story so entertaining. The fact that it happened mostly at spring training makes it all the more worth telling. You see in my line of work, the story of how an item is obtained can be just a fascinating as the item itself. And this tale begins with a suicide and a pair of pants.

February in Indiana is dark, dreary and practically unbearable—unless you like cold and snow and grey cloudy days with no end. Those people who love snow usually are complaining we don't get as much as Minnesota, while people like me are counting down the days until spring and March Madness. Most Hoosiers simply endure February as if it were the calendar equivalent of waiting in line. Fate may have given us a few things to entertain us along the way like college basketball and Valentine's Day, but you're still just waiting in line. For four weeks.

So, I should not have been the least bit perturbed when the phone rang and the voice on the other end was offering to disrupt the cold, grey misery that is February with an adventure. Still, I was in hibernation mode and couldn't abide my misery being disturbed. We're such ungrateful creatures, aren't we?

The disruption came from a colorful old friend in Phoenix.

"Quick?"

"Yes, who's this?"

"It's Rainbow." Rainbow Ruben is half Jewish and half Hawaiian. He is half crazy too, but I don't want to confuse you with math.

"Do you remember Eddie Sloane?"

"Of course I do. I found his pants."

"His what? Never mind. He's dead."

"That's awful. Heart attack?"

"Suicide."

"Oh, I'm really sorry to hear that. I always liked Eddie. Any idea why?"

"That prick killed Eddie," Rainbow replied.

"I thought you just said Eddie killed Eddie."

"Don't be a schmuck. Eddie was driven to this. The son of a bitch killed him, even if he wasn't holding the gun." In his voice, I could hear the hurt. Rainbow had lost a dear friend.

"Who killed him?"

"I'll tell you when you get here."

"I'm not coming down for another two weeks."

"You're leaving tonight. The boys arranged everything."

My doorbell rang. "Hold on, someone's at the door."

"That would be the driver."

"Driver," I asked as I answered the door.

Sure enough, I opened it to a man, dressed in a black suit, who announced, "I'll be driving you to the airport, sir. Are you ready to go?"

"No, I'm not ready to go. In fact you're two weeks early." I was going to Phoenix in two weeks to take in some games and attend a large memorabilia convention and auction.

"My paperwork says tonight," said the driver.

"Get down here, you moron," Rainbow barked into the phone.

"What exactly do you want me to do?"

"Figure out who killed him and why."

"You said you already knew who killed him."

"I do, I just want you to prove it and figure out why."

"But I'm not a detective!"

"Doesn't matter. You find things. You uncover things. It's the same set of skills."

"And on whose dime am I working?"

"Ours. The Fungo Society will pay your expenses. Now get your ass down to first." That was one of Rainbow's favorite sayings. There would be no more arguing as he had hung up the phone.

I sat down in a stadium seat from the Polo Grounds— my decorating style could be called early ballpark. I didn't spend a lot of time at home anyway, so I hadn't really put a lot of effort into things like decorating or furniture.

"Sir?" The driver was still standing in the doorway.

"What time is my flight," I asked.

"In two hours. It's a chartered jet."

"Chartered jet?" These guys are serious—and well funded. "Guess I should suit up. Looks like I'm going to pinch hit."

"Sir," he asked.

"Never mind. I'll get my stuff." He struck me as a soccer guy.

It wasn't hard to leave Indiana two weeks early. Phoenix was warm without a flake of snow in sight. The

Fungo Society would be paying for the hotel and the food, and I figured I could play detective for them for a couple of weeks before the big show. Easy, right?

I should have known better. Nothing is easy in this life. And when a crazy ex-ballplayer tells you he thinks a crime has been committed, one probably has. Of course, it might not be the crime you think.

Rainbow didn't waste much time with pleasantries when he picked me up at the airport. "Aloha, Quick. Take a look at this." He handed me a manila folder. In it was a recent picture of Eddie wearing his old uniform.

"When was this taken," I asked.

"He took it the morning he shot himself. Used a tripod and a timer."

"Where did you get it?"

"I spoke with his daughter after we heard the news and she asked me to get a copy of it from the police. They weren't going to release it to her right away."

"So, how did you get it from the police?

"Do you remember Slick Rollins?"

I had to think for a moment. "Utility infielder from Seattle? Wore those crazy sideburns in the late '70s?

"Yeah, that's him. His son is a detective on the Phoenix police force. So, I called in a favor."

By now we were at Rainbow's car. I threw my bags in the trunk and settled into the passenger seat to study the picture. Eddie Sloane was wearing his 1969 Kansas City Royals jersey and a well-worn cap. The jersey was snug around the waist since he had put on weight since he last wore it in a game. I say wore it in a game, because this was no Mitchell & Ness reproduction of a vintage jersey (although they do exquisite work). No, this was a real game-used jersey, as were the pants and cleats he was wearing.

Rainbow continued, "Eddie put that uniform on, took the picture of himself then pulled a revolver out of a box he used to keep under the bed and shot himself."

"Why did he bother to take the picture?"

"I don't know. I was hoping you could guess something from it. His daughter couldn't explain it and the police didn't seem all that interested. I guess they think that the fact that he killed himself shows he wasn't thinking clearly, so they don't think there is any particular reason to analyze it.

I started to put the photo back in the folder. "I guess they're right."

"No, they aren't. I don't believe that and neither do you. There is something weird about that. Some message he was trying to convey to us or he wouldn't have done it. He didn't take that picture for himself—he pulled the trigger right afterwards. He was never going to see it."

I pulled it back out and studied the photo as we continued to drive. It took a few minutes, but I finally found something unusual. "Hey, Rainbow, did you notice he's wearing a jersey under the jersey?"

"No, I didn't. Is that significant?"

"I don't know. But it is weird. Most guys wear a T-shirt, or baseball sleeves underneath. But I can see just enough of the piping and top button to tell that there is definitely a jersey under his Royals jersey."

"I wonder if his daughter noticed." Rainbow said.

"We should ask her. If she missed it, maybe a fresh look might help her tell us what Eddie was trying to say with this picture."

***

I have a storefront, open four days per week in the Nora neighborhood of Indianapolis. Of course, you're wondering why on earth would anyone put such a shop in Indianapolis, since there is no Major League Baseball team there. But Indianapolis does have a rich baseball tradition and these are the days of the Internet and overnight shipping. A buyer and a seller need not be in the same zip code.

I also do a lot of private transactions, as it were. Serious collectors will send me on an errand, as I like to call them, and I will flush out a prized jersey or bat. I occasionally dabble in the other sports, but baseball is where I belong.

Due to my many errands, I have Kevin to run the shop in my absence. Lately he runs the shop when I am there, but I don't mind because I know it's in good hands. Kevin is a 26-year-old student at Indiana University-Purdue University Indianapolis. The reason he is 26 and still a student is he has changed majors four times—each with progressively worse prospects for employment. At present, this fact is irrelevant to Kevin. He's surrounded by cards, collectibles, and artifacts every day and loves to debate the occasional SABR member who wanders into the shop—SABR being the Society of American Baseball Research. I'm a member and the guys are always coming in to settle some argument about an 1883 era shortstop who may or may not have stolen six bases in a game—that type of thing. Kevin, though not a member, is as knowledgeable about the game as anyone.

Kevin called me as Rainbow and I were leaving the airport. Eddie was a client and a friend. I had found his pants—his game pants, that is. He had managed to swipe his jersey before retiring but didn't have the matching pants. It took me six months and I had almost given up. But I have tipsters everywhere and a friend who runs a uniform blog used the power of social media and his thousands of followers to sniff them out. Kevin also chased down leads for me as well and really liked Eddie.

"I just heard about Eddie. Are you thinking of going down for the funeral?"

"I'm already here. The Fungos flew me down."

"Wow, that was fast. You coming back or are you going to stay down there? That's an extra two weeks."

"Yeah, but they have a job for me to do while I'm here, so I may not be back. You think you can hold down the fort?"

"Sure, but weren't you going to bring some of this stuff down for the auction? Do you want me to ship it?"

"We'll see. I'm not sure what I'm in for here, so we'll play this one by ear."

"What do they have you looking for?"

"Not the usual job. They think Eddie's suicide is a murder."

"We know it's a murder!"

"Is that Rainbow?"

"Yes."

"Tell him I said hi."

"He says hi."

"Is that kid going to graduate this year or start another major?"

"Tell him I'm thinking about switching to law school since my boss is going to be solving murders now."

"Look, do the two of you want to have your own discussion and stop wasting my time?"

"Sorry. Did you wake up on the wrong side of the bed?"

"He's in Phoenix in February, kid. He's got nothing to be crabby about."

"I'll talk with you later, Kevin."

"Wait! What about the pants?"

"What about them?"

"You should get them back before his relatives auction them off. The jersey too."

"I don't know, it's a little soon."

"Better you than some shark that wants to profit off suicide clothes. Later." He hung up.

I shuddered at the thought of some dealer getting his hands on Eddie's pants and jersey and selling them. Game-used was one thing, but suicide-used seemed macabre to me.

Reuben asked, "Is that kid ever going to graduate?"

"Jeez, I hope not," I responded. "Who else am I going to get to run the place while I'm running around spring training?"

Chapter Two

Rainbow came by the hotel early and we left to get some breakfast before the meeting. The Fungo Society met monthly in a conference room in the same hotel I was staying, so after breakfast we returned to the Peoria Palace Hotel & Conference Center. I'm not sure if it was ever a palace, but it passed nicely as a conference center. That's not to say that it wasn't a nice hotel, but I did notice some peculiar things in the parking lot upon my return.

When I pulled into the parking lot it was a cross section of life: spring breakers, monster trucks, and a van that looked like it had broken down in the parking lot in the 80's and never moved. A dirty film covered the windows and a tiny puff of smoke came out of the back window every so often.

I entered the lobby and found Rainbow along with Scooter Williams, the former Cleveland shortstop chatting up the assistant manager of the hotel. She was a pretty woman, somewhere around 29 years old. Rainbow has a daughter who is about the same age. But age is just state of mind to a guy like Scooter. He still thinks he can hit a Major League fastball. As I walked up to them, he was making his move. "What time do you get off work today?"

Rainbow rolled his eyes and told me, "rescue him before there is an incident. I've got to hit the bathroom."

She resisted, "Oh, I don't know. I may have to work late."

"I can swing by late. I'm new in town, why don't you show me the sites?" A complete lie. Scooter has lived here since the '80s.

"Hi, Scooter," I interjected.

"Hey kid. Just a minute," Scooter told me before turning back to the assistant manager. "What do you say?"

"Sir, I'm really not supposed to date the hotel guests."

"Guests? You think I would stay in this dump? No, offense, mind you."

She was offended.

"But, I'm just visiting my friend. I'm not staying here."

"Scooter let's go up ..."

My intrusion irritated him. "In a minute, kid."

"So, you see it's perfectly okay for you to go out with me."

"Pardon me, miss, is this man bothering you?" I asked.

"Well, I ..."

"Bothering her? I'm just trying to be friendly."

"I'm sorry, he gets a little pushy when he hasn't had his nap."

"My nap?"

She looked back at me. "Yes, his nap. Now if you have any ideas how a guy like me can keep a senior like him entertained in town, here's my card, I would love to discuss them with you over dinner."

I winked and grabbed Scooter by the arm and pulled him away. "What the… did you just…"

I walked him away and looked back over my shoulder. She was still looking at me and smiling. "Call me," I mouthed.

As we got on the elevator, Scooter was angry. "You just stole my date for tonight." Rainbow met us as the elevator door was about to close. "Rainbow, he stole my date."

"Come on, Scooter. You didn't have a chance," he replied.

"I could have shown her a better time than either of you," he responded."

"She didn't look like the blue plate buffet type."

Scooter was fuming. "Hey, you're on our payroll down here. You need to start acting like it. Show some respect."

"That's why I rescued you from making a fool of yourself," I said.

Rainbow laughed as Scooter complained all the way up the elevator.

***

We met in a small conference room on the third floor of the hotel. There were 15 guys ranging in age from mid-50s up to 74. This was the Fungo Society. In years gone by, this group might have attracted a crowd of autograph hounds and picture takers. But there weren't any hall of famers in the group. These were mostly everyday players. Guys who scrapped out a living in the big leagues, then went on to lead regular lives. Most stayed connected to the game in some way: coaches, scouts, and various front office jobs. Yet most of the guys had retired even from these gigs. They had time on their hands and they needed something to focus their energies upon. Eddie's death had given them that focus. They were loaded for bear.

"This is Mr. Quick," Rainbow introduced me.

I looked around the room. Some of the faces were familiar, even guys I had done business with. Some were new to me, but reminded me of some old baseball card. "Gentlemen, how can I be of service," I asked.

"We want you to pin Eddie's death on Byrne," said the first to answer, Hal Rankin. Hal had played shortstop for Kansas City and Texas.

"I'm pretty sure, the police have ruled it a suicide," I responded. "And who is Byrne?"

"Oh, that's horse shit," fired someone to my left. I looked at him and recognized former catcher Wally Lutz.

Another shouted, "Eddie didn't kill himself."

"Well, he did pull the trigger," I replied.

"Yes, but that son of a bitch drove him to it," answered Scooter.

"Eddie would never have done that on his own," said a man on my left. He looked familiar. I was trying to place his name with my memory of baseball cards (something I do a lot when meeting former players) and all I could think of was the word "Prophet." Maybe that was his nickname?

"Do you believe someone was in the room with him, forcing him to shoot himself?" I asked.

"No, of course not. But we all believe,"—Hal paused and looked around the room—"every one of us, that Byrne killed Eddie. He double-crossed him. Drove him to bankruptcy, and then took his prized possession."

"Byrne who?" I asked.

"Byrne the developer. Byrne Commercial Properties? Byrne Family Homes? Any of this ring a bell?" asked Scooter.

"Carl Byrne?" I was surprised and slightly puzzled. "You think he killed Eddie," I asked.

"Exactly," Scooter replied and they all seemed to lean back on their chairs as if the matter had been solved.

"What do you expect me to do?"

"Yeah, Ruben, what the hell did we bring this guy down here for?" asked Hal.

"Are you a cop." asked Prophet. I remembered now. Prophet was Moses Gable. He actually became a Baptist Preacher after his playing days. I guess your name can predict your life path. Of course, he wasn't much of a "holy man" having around this lot!

"No."

"Are you a detective?" asked Wally.

"No, I deal in artifacts," I responded.

"Then why are you here?" This was a tough crowd.

"I found Eddie's pants."

Someone shouted from behind me, "he's wearing his pants?" Teddy Kramer was 74 years old. He played for the Mets and had a brief stint with the Royals. That's where he met Eddie. Not everyone in the room had played for the Royals; it wasn't a Fungo Society requirement. But they all had connected in some way during their playing or front office careers.

"No, you old fart. They shared pants," said Hal.

"Didn't know Eddie was that way," Teddy replied. Does his wife know?"

"What way?"

The old man responded, "You know, one of the gays."

"One of the gays?"

"Eddie's not gay, Mr. Quick just found his pants."

"Found his pants?" asked Teddy.

Teddy continued, "Why did you hire a guy who can't even find his own pants?"

"This is hopeless," I muttered.

"Teddy, Mr. Quick found Eddie's actual game pants from his Royals days."

"Oh, why didn't you say so? Go on."

"Uh, thank you. Seriously, guys," I turned to Rainbow. "Just what is it you want me to do?"

"You're smart and resourceful," Rainbow replied. "Either find a way to help us pin Eddie's death on Byrne or help us get revenge."

"Revenge? You want me to help you kill him? Seems a little drastic." I said.

"No, we don't want to kill him," Rainbow said.

"I do," said Hank.

"Okay, Hank does. But the rest of us just want to ruin him like he ruined Eddie.

"Embarrass him. That's what Eddie did." Teddy yelled.

Scooter responded, "Yeah, and now Eddie's dead."

"What if we figured out how to ruin and/or embarrass him without him knowing it was us?" asked Rainbow.

"Yeah, I like that idea," Teddy said. Several of the men chimed in their approval.

"Quick, can you do it," Scooter asked.

"Do what? I don't even know what we're talking about."

"We're talking about bringing down the empire of Mr. Byrne. Pay attention, you putz." Rainbow was getting chippy.

"And how do you propose we do that?" I asked. "Besides real estate, what is this guy into?"

"You mean besides bats. That's where his real fortune lies."

"Wait a minute. You're telling me the Byrne we're going after is the same Byrne from the bat company?"

Everyone looked at me like I was an idiot. Of course I had heard of Byrne bats and of course I could pick out an authentic one at an auction. It was just that I had never made the connection that the Byrne that Eddie was mixed up with would be the same one who owned the bat company.

Byrne Bats was formed in the early 50's. They had been on the field of Major League Baseball since 1959 and had a minor piece of the pie. Louisville Slugger is still the main player, along with Adirondack, Mizuno. I soon learned about a new player joining them this year: Mine Bats.

Carl Byrne had inherited the business from his father. Byrne had a caustic reputation. Born into money, he was brash and headstrong. Still, it didn't make sense that he would screw Eddie over. I didn't doubt these guys that it happened, I just felt there was a lot I still needed to know.

"Taking on Carl Byrne is not going to be an easy task. You know that don't you?"

"You chicken?" shouted Teddy. "Put a cup on you sissy!"

"I don't think I'm going to need a cup to take on Byrne."

"What do you think you will need," asked Ruben.

"Now, I didn't say I would take the gig."

"Take the gig, you're here on our dime, Quick. We're paying you by the day. You're in this thing."

At this point I thought I should just agree. These guys would lose interest in (and memory of) what we were talking about by the time the blue plate special was served tonight at whatever Denny's they were planning on going to at 5 p.m.

"Alright, alright. I'll take the gig."

"Wait a minute, why are we risking our necks? This could get dangerous," asked Hal.

"Every man in this room owes a debt to Eddie."

"I don't," he replied.

Rainbow started to grow angry. "Every man. Especially you."

Hal remained stubborn. "I do not."

"The hell you don't. He introduced you to your wife."

"She left me."

Scooter chimed in. "You cheated on her."

"Well, yeah there's that."

Rainbow continued. "Come on you guys, we owe this to Eddie. One of our guys has been knocked down by the opposing pitcher. It's up to us to defend his honor."

"Anybody else not sure?" asked Scooter.

A few hands went up. Rainbow ignored them "Fine, let's go. Everyone pile into their cars and follow me."

"Where are we going?"

"Not far. Less than a mile from here is all the reason any of you need to do this for Eddie."

I'm not sure what power Ruben had over these guys but they all followed him out of the conference room and out into the elevators. We piled into one, making it very cozy and stuffy. Out we came on the ground floor and the guys shuffled along towards the main lobby doors. I shot a wink to the receptionist who was looking at this curious crew and the one thirty-year-old guy who was with them.

For a moment, I considered ditching the guys and staying with her. But she was on the job, so any leisurely pursuits I might have been planning for us would have to wait. Fifteen guys piled into four cars and followed Rainbow. True to his word we followed him for only a mile before he turned into a nursing home. The Cozy Cactus Senior Living Center was well manicured and inviting. But it was still a nursing home and that made me a little uneasy. I liked old people, and I was enjoying the insanity of the Fungo Society. But nursing homes are a little too close to the end, if you know what I mean.

Ruben led us into the lobby and an attendant came to meet us. He was a little unnerved by the large group of older men walking in. Maybe he feared it was a mass check-in. But Ruben assured him we were harmless and he buzzed us into the Alzheimer's ward. Beyond the secure wall was the world of Alzheimer's. For those who have never experienced it, it is soul crushing. Some rooms were deathly quiet. Patients didn't stir, struggling with the final stages of the disease. In the hall, we were greeted by a man who asked us where the bus stop was. I told him I didn't think the bus came this way.

"Sir, can you tell me where the bus stop is?"

"I don't think it comes this way," I said.

"Can you give me a ride? I'm late for work."

"I can't take you, I don't have my car. But I will see if I can find somebody who can," I replied.

I knew he wasn't late for anything. He was a patient, condemned to spending his final days in this place. That's not to say the people who worked here weren't kind and compassionate. It was clean, and even decorated in a fun way. I noticed a framed jersey or two as we went along. Somebody had donated the memorabilia. I thought it was a strange place to have baseball jerseys, but we were in the spring training capital of the Southwest.

When Rainbow brought the guys to the nursing home, most expected Sally to be the same woman they knew in their playing days. Back then she was full of zest. She was always moving, always smiling, and never seemed to have a bad day. She wasn't just Eddie's wife. She was the team mom, the matchmaker, the voice of reason and wisdom. They thought they were going to see that same bundle of life, maybe just a little worn down by the years. Slower, but still moving.

What they got was something completely different. Sally Sloane was in her seventh year of battling the disease, Ruben explained. "He came here most days and read to her. Over the last few months, she started to go downhill. Eddie didn't want to bring her here, but he couldn't afford to care for her at home with a visiting nurse, and he wasn't physically able to help her bathe and go to the bathroom. It was that bastard Byrne that put her here. Of course, she probably would have had to come here eventually, but Eddie losing everything sped it up. She probably could have stayed at home another year."

"Does she recognize anybody?"

"Maybe a few."

At this point Sally woke up. She looked at Ruben and smiled. She looked at the empty chair and spoke. "Eddie dear, that nice Jewish fellow is here."

"Hello, Sally," Ruben asked. "How are you feeling today?"

"I'm alright. I'm thinking about getting off the couch and tending the flowers." She looked over at the empty seat. "Eddie, don't you think we need to tend the flowers?"

"Sally, do you remember Bobby Voight?"

"Did he play for the Royals?"

"I sure did," Bobby said. "Great to see you, Sally."

"Good to see you too, dear."

"Eddie, wasn't he a better hitter than you?"

Everyone laughed. "All of us were better hitters than Eddie."

"Not you, Ruben. You couldn't hit water if you fell out of a boat." She still had glimpses of a sharp wit. Rainbow got a little red in the face.

"What are all you boys doing here? Is there a game today?"

"No, Sally," Rainbow said. "We've got the day off."

"When do we play New York? I always loved going to New York."

"Next month, I think Sally."

"That will be fun. Eddie, do you think we should tend the flowers," she said again to the empty chair.

"Do you miss Eddie, Sally?"

"Oh, no he's not missing. Just went to get the mail I think."

"I'm sure he'll be right back," Rainbow said. I shot him a look.

Most of the guys got choked up. They now knew that Sally had no idea her Eddie was dead. Oh, sure, I'm certain she had been told. But the fragility of her mind and the destruction caused by the disease wouldn't let it stick.

The nurse who had escorted us to the room recognized the shock of the men who knew Sally as a young woman. It was a daily occurrence for the nurse: Seeing the faces of friends and loved ones who expect the person they used to know. First it's shock. Then, they look at the nurse as if she has brought them to the wrong room.

But there is no other room and the person they used to know is a shadow. The lives of people in the last stages of Alzheimer's are vapor trails. You may see the evidence of someone who passed this way, but they are increasingly not with us anymore.

Occasionally though, there are random neural firings that defy logic and confound doctors and scientists. Even when all recognition of people has passed, there are echoes of memories that manifest in strange ways. In her healthier days, Sally was the guardian of clean language. She always let the boys know when their cursing crossed the line.

"Eddie's life insurance won't pay out because he committed suicide. If we can't prove Byrne killed him, or at least get some of the money back that he swindled out of him, she will have to move to a dumpy retirement home in Marysville next month. Her daughter won't be able to afford to keep her here. Eddie wanted her to spend her last days here."

Hal grew angry. "That no good son of a ..."

Before he got the words out, Sally raised her hand, just as she had done countless times when they all played together. One hand, straight in the air, palm facing Hal. She might not have recognized him, but she knew where that sentence was going and she would have none of it. In the old days, the guys would always make fun of the offending party. Nobody ever crossed her and said whatever word was coming out of his mouth when she raised her hand.

This time they didn't taunt. They didn't tease. The memories of the old days enveloped them. Each of them fought back tears. Silently, one by one, they retreated into the hallway. Rainbow didn't have to cajole them any more. They were in.

Chapter Three

"Did you ditch the old man?" I heard a familiar voice call from behind me as I returned to my hotel. A sultry Spanish accented female voice. Rainbow dropped me off at the hotel after the trip to the nursing home. It was the woman Scooter had tried to pick up earlier.

"As a matter of fact, I did."

"Too bad," she flirted. "I'm just finishing my shift and I was going to show you both around town.

I walked to the counter. She leaned forward towards me. "He's down for a nap and we really don't want to disturb him. Maybe you should just give me the tour."

"What's your name?"

"Quick."

"Nice to meet you Mr. Quick. I'm Ramona." She extended her hand to shake.

"Just Quick. It's a pleasure to meet you."

"I'll be done in about 15 minutes. Meet me back here and I will show you how to enjoy Phoenix."

I won't clutter your mind with the illicit details of what happened that night. Suffice it to say, she really did not show me how to enjoy Phoenix. But she did show me how to enjoy Ramona. And that of course was my first truly big mistake in this adventure, a fact I realized quickly the next morning when I came down to the lobby for breakfast.

"Mr. Quick." Ramona's voice didn't sound sultry today. It sounded perturbed. "You have a message from some woman."

Ever notice how women say, "some woman" and tilt or twitch their head as they say it? It's always with a hint of loathing mixed with jealousy. I had been in Phoenix all of one day and one rather amorous night. And now Ramona was saying "some woman" like she owned me.

I approached the counter and smiled. "Probably the auction company. May I see it?"

She handed me the note, but I didn't need to read it as Ramona quoted it from memory. "She said she wants to meet you here, in the lobby at eleven. Says it's urgent."

"Urgent?"

"Yes, she claims to be the daughter of Mr. Sloane and says you know her."

The "know her" was said with even more loathing than the "some woman." I had seen a few pictures—old ones at that—of Eddie's daughter, but wouldn't be able to pick her out of a lineup.

"She says she has a job for you to do?" Ramona rolled her eyes as if the job entailed performing passionate acts upon the woman who left the message.

"Seriously, I don't know her."

"I hope you're not planning any funny business with this slut."

"She is not a slut."

"So you do know her."

"No, I just mean I'm pretty certain she is not coming here for sex." This started a volley of what I can only assume were expletives but since I don't speak Spanish, I can't say with certainty.

I tried to interrupt, offer a few reassurances, but Ramona just kept getting louder. Finally, I tried to shout over her Spanish cursing by yelling, "You're the only person in this hotel that I want to have sex with!"

At this moment, I remembered we were in a hotel lobby in the middle of the morning on a busy weekday. And it was also at this moment that I felt the eyes of someone behind me. I turned around and there was a family of four: Mr. and Mrs. Middle America with their two kids. Mom covered her eight-year-old daughter's ears. Dad was red-faced, but I thought I detected just a hint of an approving grin. His son was picking his nose.

I stumbled and stammered out a few "excuse me's" and "I'm sorry's" but they were woefully inadequate. So, I left Ramona with the unenviable task of apologizing for the scene and convincing the family that this was a respectable hotel, despite the presence of people like me.

After breakfast, I went back up to my room to shower, put on some clean clothes, and check email. Just before eleven, I went downstairs to stake out a place to meet Jessica Sloane. I wasn't anticipating having any romantic inclinations toward Eddie's daughter, but I didn't want Ramona interrupting the proceedings especially if there was money involved. No sense risking the loss of a client due to the behavior of a very possessive hotel manager.

When I got off the elevator, Ramona was nowhere in sight. I quickly found a spot that gave me a view of the front door while being obscured from the front desk. Two chairs and a small table tucked away in a corner. A perfect place to have a chat, do business and not have jealous eyes upon us. Plus if Ramona did decide to intercede—which I was most certain she would—I could see her coming.

Of course, like most things when it comes to women, I was wrong on both counts. I was wrong about Ramona trying to interrupt. And I was wrong about having any romantic notions about Jessica. How was I to know she would show up looking like she did?

What is it about a woman's legs that make a man weak in the knees? A great set of legs, that is. There are all kinds, of course, but the ones attached to Jessica Sloane gave me vertigo. She entered the hotel lobby and marched right towards me. The male business travelers, spring training fans, and hotel staff all paused to watch the show. Business blazer on top and short skirt below, five-inch heels that made her tower over everyone. Jessica dominated the room like her dad used to dominate a groundball.

Thank God Ramona didn't see her. I found out later she was answering to her boss for a complaint about an outburst from a family that checked in that morning.

I summoned the strength to rise and shake Jessica's hand. "Mr. Quick," she asked.

"That's what it says on my drivers license." Did that really come out of my mouth?

We both sat down.

"So, you have a secret identity?" I liked her sharp response.

"Oh, more than one. I find they come in handy when trying to unearth artifacts."

"You mean like role playing." She crossed those legs.

I had to pause for the lump in my throat to clear. "Something like that. What role can I play for you?"

She leaned forward. "Let's start with detective."

"Okay."

"I want you to find my father's jersey. Byrne bought it at auction. I want it back."

"Shouldn't be hard to track down. I doubt he has already sold it to another collector." I replied.

"He hasn't. It's his prized possession."

"Then it won't be easy to acquire."

"That's why I'm hiring you. They say you're the best." This look wasn't as flirty. She seemed sincere and businesslike. When she talks business, she means business. I, on the other hand, was completely turned on.

"If you don't mind my asking, why does the jersey of a mostly forgotten ballplayer from the late '60s matter to Byrne?"

"Do you know much about my father's former partner?"

"Not a lot. Enlighten me."

"He's ruthless and cruel. Don't let all the civic awards fool you. He ruined my father, took him for everything he had."

"How so?"

"He used my father's name and money to start construction of an office park in Scottsdale," she said.

"I get why some companies would want to have a celebrity endorsement, but no offense, Eddie had mostly slipped into obscurity. It's not like he's Dave Winfield or George Brett."

"You're right, my father wasn't a household name anymore. And that's the kind of person Byrne targets. He convinced my dad that people did still see him as a celebrity and stroked his ego to get to his wallet. Guys who miss the cheers of adoring fans and have a little cash to invest are ripe for a fall."

"But if the real estate deal went south, Byrne lost money too, right?"

"Not really. With Dad's money funding the start-up and it being organized as a corporation, he hid the fact that he didn't actually invest any of his own money. He got loans on my dad's name and credit and even made sure my dad signed the personal guarantees. When the economy tanked, so did the project. Nine out of ten companies that had agreed to move into the commercial space simply walked away from their deposits."

"And Eddie couldn't recoup any money from Byrne?"

"Not a penny. And nothing that he did was technically illegal. But he made sure that if there was going to be any adverse results to the venture, my Dad bore the brunt of them. My dad realized he was partly to blame for listening to Byrne's flattery and not having an attorney properly vet the deal. Still, he came from a world where you don't screw your teammates. And that made him angry."

"So where does the jersey come in," I asked.

"Dad spiraled down as he tried to deal with the losses and my mom's health issues. He began drinking too much and one night after a few too many he went to a civic dinner where Byrne was being honored."

"This doesn't sound good."

"No, it wasn't. My dad called him out in front of a couple hundred of the city's richest and powerful people. It even made the local news. After my father embarrassed him, Byrne threatened to get even. He sent some nasty letters via his attorney, but never followed through until he bought that jersey out from under us at the auction."

"I recall that your father once had a Babe Ruth jersey. What happened to that? It was worth a fortune," I said.

"There wasn't a Babe Ruth jersey in the items that went to auction. How much was it worth?"

"Quite a bit. It was a 1938 Brooklyn Dodgers jersey."

"Dodgers? I thought Ruth played for the Yankees," Jessica asked.

"He did, but after retiring, he spent one season as a first base coach for the Dodgers. By most accounts, they were just paying him to come to the stadium and be himself. They didn't seriously consider him for a future manager, which is what he wanted. So, it only lasted one year."

"How did my father get the jersey?"

"Eddie, said he got it from the equipment manager of the Dodgers. Said they were cousins."

"Uncle Sal?"

"Yeah, Sal Cordello."

"I knew he was from Brooklyn, never knew he worked for the Dodgers."

"I inspected it myself, probably seven or eight years ago. It was legit. Amazing shape. If it's gone, what a loss."

"I still have all his records. Maybe I can find something that will give us a clue as to where it's at."

"So, which jersey do you want me to find?" I asked.

"Both, of course," she said.

"And what are you willing to pay?"

"I'll give you $1,000 for recovering my father's jersey and ten percent of whatever we can sell the Ruth jersey for."

"Plus expenses?"

"Plus expenses. Sure, but what kind of expenses are there in an endeavor such as this?"

The sound of Ramona's heels made me notice her walk across the lobby trying to spy while trying to look as if she were not spying. Glancing back at Jessica, I said, "oh, there's a lot of legwork. Lots of legwork."

She recrossed her own legs. "Well, I will trust you to be reasonable with the expenses."

"I'm sure you will find it well worth the cost," I said.

"Getting back to your father's jersey, I do have some questions. First, why was it in an auction?"

"After my father lost all his money and was forced to sell almost all that he owned. My plan was to buy the jersey, along with many of his other possessions and give them back to him."

"Did Byrne buy other items that belonged to your dad?"

"No, just the jersey. I'm not made of cash, so bidding on the other things was eating up my budget for the day. When we got to the jersey, he was hell-bent on outbidding me."

"Why that jersey? It's game used and authentic, but it's not like your dad was a Hall of Famer—no offense."

"No, I get it. It shouldn't have made most people even notice. But I think he knew it was important to my father. While the bidding was going on, he saw the pain on my father's face. With each bid higher than mine, he took more pleasure. I know it's not worth much. I'm certain he bought it for spite"

"How much did it ultimately go for?"

"Five thousand dollars."

"Five thousand? That's a lot of spite!"

"Enough spite to make my dad want to kill himself."

"You know his Fungo Society friends think Byrne did this on purpose, knowing that he would kill himself."

"I wouldn't put it past him, if he knew that's how far it would make my father go. No, I would say in his evil mind, the suicide was just a bonus."

"Regardless, those guys are determined to get revenge."

"They'll get hurt—talk them out of it. Some of them were very good to our family. I wouldn't want any of them to get hurt," she said.

"Me? They won't listen to me."

"They respect you. Isn't that why you're here?"

"I'm here, because they think I'm like a detective who can find a way to pin your dad's death on Byrne."

"You're not a detective."

"That's what I said. But they seem to think I can find anything."

"Can you," she asked as she got up to leave.

"When it comes to baseball artifacts, yes."

She shook my hand and said, "I sure hope so." I watched her walk away and she turned and smiled. "By the way, what did you find for my father?"

Just then, the mom and daughter from this morning's incident came around the corner.

"I found his pants," I answered and winked at the mom.

Chapter Four

The next day was the first of March and that meant Opening Day for spring training games. Rainbow and Scooter agreed to join me and we took the 101 to Camelback Ranch to see the Padres and White Sox. It was sunny and warm, completely indistinguishable from the last 100 days in Phoenix, I imagined. Some people can't handle the lack of a change of seasons. More power to them. I could go my whole life without seeing another snowflake and be just dandy.

Some people will tell you that Arizona has seasons, but remember that peyote is easy to come by here. There may be differing degrees of warm and sunny—but it's always warm and sunny. No danger of a snowstorm in Phoenix.

Camelback Ranch is home of the Dodgers and White Sox. It's not hard to see why the Dodgers left Vero Beach, Florida, after 50 years to come to this place. Not only is it closer geographically to Los Angeles, but the setting is the best I have seen in all of the Cactus League. The two camps are separated by a lake with waterfalls, gorgeous landscaping and friendly, helpful staff along the way.

Even though I was here for a purpose, it's hard not to get caught up in baseball fandom, especially on Opening Day. Scooter and Rainbow wanted to chat up some of the retired ladies who volunteer at the complex, so we agreed to meet up later at the game. I was wandering the pathways between the various practice fields when I came across a large group of people who were waiting for autographs. I talked with a guy named Manny who lives across the street from the complex. Every day in March, he is out here with an old photo album collecting autographs. He showed me some of the ones he had collected with pride.

The line of people waiting for autographs spanned the generations, from young children to retirees. It warmed my heart just to look at them. I was particularly impressed with long-time White Sox announcer and former player himself Hawk Harrelson. He patiently signed autographs and chatted with the people for a long time. Most of the Sox players signed for a while as well. Some just did a few baseballs and quickly made for the clubhouse.

An affable young man from San Diego struck up a conversation. He had moved to Phoenix two years ago for the lower cost of living. Now he worked as a guide at the ballpark, along with other jobs after spring training was over. His name was Jose, and he wore a neoprene sleeve on one arm to protect him from the sun. The other arm wasn't covered, which I found strange. He also wore a large hat with a wide brim all around. It looked like something a farmer might wear in the fields.

On my way to the Dodgers side of the complex, I met a man named David from Buffalo. He moved to Phoenix after the Blizzard of '78 and never went back. I can't blame him. After several decades of supervising a manufacturing plant in a Phoenix suburb, his job moved overseas. Now he works at the park.

"It keeps me busy, but I want to work full-time," David said. "Who's going to hire me at 63? You here to see the international game?"

"No, I was looking for someone and I think they're watching a game back this way."

"Probably the French National Team. They're playing the Dodgers Single A players. It started about 10 minutes ago. Lots of people have passed by here on their way to that game."

"Thanks for the tip," I said.

"Lots of old ballplayers down there too. Have a good day."

I wondered if I would end up working at a ballpark when I retired. Seemed like a pretty easy gig.

Terry Franklin was there talking with Tommy Lasorda. Terry is a scout for the Milwaukee organization. I run in to him from time to time. He calls me Hoosier for some reason. I've never quite figured out if it's meant to be endearing or derogatory.

David was right; there were a lot of people watching the game. It seemed that one older husband and wife were the only fans of the French team. The rest were there to see the Dodgers minor leaguers. The setting was like a little league game. The Dodgers side of the field was lined with golf carts filled with men I'm assuming were coaches of various levels.

There was a small set of bleachers, but it was crammed with coaches, scouts, and players who weren't playing in this particular game. Fans lined the field with lawn chairs, too. You can walk right up to the fence, and very little separated you from the players. Still, most fans are polite and don't press for autographs while the game is underway.

After watching a few innings I left for the main complex where the Major League guys would be playing. Scooter whizzed by in a golf cart driven by a lady about his age. They stopped in front of me and backed up. "You want a lift?"

"Sure," I answered. "And who might this young lady be?"

"Don't get any ideas, Quick. This is my lady friend, Loretta."

Loretta was 70, sharp as a tack and drove like a golf cart like it was the Indy 500. "Hold on tight, sugar," she laughed as we took off and followed the winding path to the stadium. "You boys have a good time now," she told us as we unloaded by the outfield gate. "Enjoy the game."

"How long have the two of you been dating?"

"Since last Christmas," Scooter replied. "I met her at the casino. We were both playing blackjack."

"How long has she been on staff here?"

"Since this place opened. She loves to drive the carts. Pretty handy to have her around when you want to get from one field to the next." Loretta would come in very handy before this Fungo adventure was over.

In the first week of March, fewer families are on Spring Break and this being a weekday, the crowd was sparse. Rainbow rejoined Scooter and me and we had our pick of seats. There were no fans behind us and just a couple of snowbirds to our left. We sat behind the Padres dugout and chatted with an usher who had very few people to ush.

Just before the first pitch, Jessica called my cell phone.

"Quick, can I talk with you for a minute?"

"Sure, what's up?"

"I'm looking over my father's books and I've found something strange. He does have a receipt for selling the Babe Ruth jersey."

"Who did he sell it to, and for how much?"

"The company name is KC Collectibles and the amount is $500,000."

"KC Collectibles, huh. I know a little about them. Is the receipt dated?"

"Yes, it says 2007."

"Okay, I'll see what I can find out about them. But it looks like that mystery is solved."

"Yes, but I think I unearthed another one." Jessica paused. "I'm not sure what to think."

"What do you mean?"

"That same year, he sold a piece of property for the same amount. I don't see how the jersey could have fetched as much money as the land and I sure don't see how the ranch he sold could have only brought in half a million dollars."

"Yeah, I'm not following the connection."

"You're at the Padres-White Sox game, right?" How did she know that?.

"Yes, the game just started."

"You're sitting in the middle of the land he sold."

"Really? That had to be worth way more than $500,000."

"I agree. Something seems off about this. That land had to be worth more than that and I can't imagine my dad taking that low of an offer. I know he made a bad deal with Byrne, but for the most part he was pretty good with money."

"Do you still want me to keep digging?"

"Maybe a few more shovels full," she answered. "Oh, and one other thing that might help. My father donated some memorabilia to the nursing home. You probably saw some of it when you visited."

"Yes, I remember seeing a few things."

"All of that will come back to me when my mother moves out or passes away. I doubt that he would have put the Ruth jersey in that collection, though. I think most of the pieces were of minimal value."

"Okay, I might go back and have a closer look. Hey, I meant to ask you something yesterday. I apologize in advance for this question. When your dad committed suicide, he was wearing a jersey under his jersey. You don't happen to know why or what jersey it was, do you?"

"I collected his things after, well, you know. I remember two jerseys. The one under his Royals jersey was his Tucson Torros jersey from his coaching days. He wore that around the house all the time, so I didn't think too much of it."

"Okay, thanks."

A jersey he wore around the house all the time didn't tell me much. I was sure when I saw the picture that he was trying to send a message. Now, it just seemed like a throwaway bit of information. Nothing he did that day made a whole lot of sense. Killing himself over a jersey? I didn't buy it. But I wasn't ready to believe it was murder.

After a few minutes of watching the game, I turned to Rainbow. "I have a question."

"Yeah?"

"How did Eddie get mixed up with Byrne in the first place?"

"When he sold the ranch," he paused and looked around us, "he and his partner walked away with a million dollars. Eddie sat on his million for a few years but then he got antsy. He wanted to get some of the boys to invest in a bowling alley, but we weren't keen on it."

"You said 'his million.' Did you mean his half?"

"His half was a million."

"Are you sure? His daughter just told me Eddie only got 500K for the ranch."

"She's mistaken. Eddie made a cool million after taxes on that deal. Saw the check myself. Hell, he even let me take my picture with it, as I hadn't ever seen a check with that many zeros." He looked at the players on the field. "For these guys it's a week's pay. For old ballplayers like myself, that's a whole lot of cash."

I thought about the discrepancy. Could Jessica have been mistaken? I thought I would check with her after the game. Scooter nudged me. "Think they're real?"

"Huh?"

He nudged me again with all the subtlety of a fastball to the head. "Those, do you think they are real?" He was of course looking at breasts. Breasts attached to a woman in her thirties wearing a black tank top and a tan miniskirt.

The breasts and the woman attached to them were attached to a rather large man who didn't seem to mind the 70-year-old man staring at his girlfriend. He did, however, mind me staring at her and raised his glasses to signal that the show was over.

They sat across the aisle and a row in front us and struck up a conversation with the three gentlemen who had quietly slipped into the row across from us. Scooter hadn't noticed them either, but of course, none of them had breasts.

"Well?"

"Well, what?"

He laughed. "Did you get a good enough look at them to tell if they were real before that bird's boyfriend shooed you off?"

"He didn't shoo me off."

"The hell he didn't. But I suppose it's for the best. Not like you can get caught up with a dame with all the work you have to do."

"You know what I like about you, Scooter?"

"What?"

"Somehow when you use words like 'bird' and 'dame' it still sounds charming. If I used those words, the PC police would shun me from decent society."

"So are you saying I'm unhip or something?" He started to seem irritated.

"No, not at all. Probably hipper than anyone at the game today."

A foul ball came our way and I heard one of the guys across the aisle say, "That was our bat." It was then that I began to take notice of them. They were studying each batter and making note of the bat brand and model used. Occasionally, they would walk down to the dugout and have a conversation with one of the players or coaches. I was just about to introduce myself when Scooter asked me to buy him a beer. By the time I returned, the bat guys had moved behind the opposing dugout.

I wanted to ask them a few questions about the bat business, or more specifically, what they knew about Byrne's business. But, some of the old timers were starting to settle in around us and I got caught up in the stories of seasons past. Hopefully, I would run into them again.

Chapter Five

On the way home from the game, I thought about
the property and the discrepancy in price. Whether
it was a half a million or a million-dollar property, it
was beyond my ability to fathom. Sure, lots of people
have investment property, but a patch of tumbleweeds
you can turn into a fortune? That's living right. Maybe
someday I will be able to turn my second property into a
fortune. Now before you think I'm of that blessed strata
of society that own vacation homes, think again. I should
be so lucky. My second property fetches neither rental
income nor the admiration of others.

I have an outhouse in Maine. Nothing else, just an
outhouse. It was a gift from my Uncle Frank. You could
call it a gift, but I'm not sure if that was the real intent.
After all, it is an outhouse and Uncle Frank was known
for his sense of humor. Some say he gave it to me for
spite. Not to spite me, but to spite his in-laws who
assumed the lakefront estate he had built over the course
of his life would be left to them. Instead, he parceled up

the property and gave some to other relatives and some friends.

His in-laws expected to get at least his house, but he left that to the grandchildren of one of his fishing buddies. For years, the in-laws had asked him to part with a small sliver of land that would give them better access to the lake from their nearby property. Frank didn't want their dock to be right next to his, so he refused. Just to spite them, he took the exact sliver of land they wanted, separated it from the rest of his estate, and left it to me. The grandchildren of Frank's fishing buddy view me as an outsider and didn't like me, so they wouldn't let me connect the sliver of land to the road running in front of their property. His in-laws, of course, were furious, so they wouldn't let me expand in their direction. So, I have a tiny strip of land, resting between the large estates of two bitter rivals. It is accessible only by boat—and I've been warned not to trespass or I will be shot.

As I said, the only structure on the property is an outhouse. There's nothing particularly marvelous or historic about the outhouse. It has no architectural significance. No famous person ever evacuated his or her bowels there. No major inventions were conceived while someone was sitting inside. It is in every way, a run-of-the-mill outhouse.

To my knowledge, no one has used the outhouse in decades. My uncle covered the seat and stored fishing gear in it. According to Uncle Frank's will, all the contents of the outhouse became mine at the time of his death. This made me laugh. My uncle warned me that I would be receiving a structure upon his passing. I hoped it was going to be the primary home. Unfortunately it wasn't to be. When the will was read, he made it a point to tell me that the walls weren't much but the view was worth a fortune.

To this day, I have no idea what Uncle Frank meant. You don't really know someone until after they die. You find out all sorts of things—quirks, hang-ups, and grudges. People tell you all the stories they were afraid to share when the person was alive.

This is what I thought we were getting with Eddie. Eddie Sloane had secrets. Those secrets didn't mean he wasn't a good guy or that all the love and devotion the Fungo Society had for him was misplaced. It just meant he was human like the rest of us. We all have skeletons in the closet. Or in the outhouse.

My uncle made his money the old fashioned way—he sold liquor. I say that because there are lots of jobs that are venerated, like doctors, lawyers, farmers, etc. Liquor store owners, not so much. They are the people that most people lift a nose at when they learn their profession. So many wealthy people of fine families will throw back a cocktail at the end of the day; they just don't want to hobnob with the people who sold it to them.

This is why despite making lots of money, my uncle never spent a lot of time trying to fit in to New England society. He never joined a country club, had no patience for golf, and wasn't particularly interested in sitting on the board of this hospital or that school. That's not to say that he wasn't charitable, he just did it in ways that most people failed to notice.

His one passion, however, was baseball. Baseball was his life and Fenway Park was his church. His saints were Williams, Yastrzemski, and Clemens. In his world, Satan's seat was in the Bronx and he employed a host of demons named DiMaggio, Mantle, Jackson, and Mattingly. Given his affection for baseball, he collected Red Sox memorabilia. I never expected to inherit any of his collection, although I did help him acquire a great deal of it. He told me all along that the collection would go to the Baseball Hall of Fame and to the Red Sox organization upon his death. He looked at himself as a curator of Red Sox history. Although his collection was large and included a great many artifacts, he always intended it to be shared with the masses someday.

When he passed away, I never expected foul play. He lived a long and full life. He had been battling lung cancer for a few years—probably the result of smoking in his twenties. Despite having quit shortly after getting married, the damage had been done. I didn't suspect foul play the day I found out he had died. I didn't suspect foul play when his relatives started sniffing around his collection. But I did suspect foul play the day I catalogued the collection for the Hall of Fame and the Red Sox and I realized that the most valuable item in his collection was missing: Babe Ruth's original contract.

I questioned the estate attorney about the item, but he found no mention of it in the will's inventory. I found this very strange, because Uncle Frank always talked about how much joy it would give him to know that the Ruth contract would be in the Hall of Fame. It was curious that it was missing. Even more curious that it wasn't listed. When I told the attorney that the contract was missing but not on the list of items, he told me that several months before his death, Frank had changed his will.

The lawyer had his assistant bring a copy of the previous version for us to review. He remembered that items were added (not, surprising since Frank never stopped collecting) but he didn't remember my uncle removing anything from the list. Apparently, whenever Frank updated his will, he would just give the attorney a new complete list of his collection and the legal assistant would update the will.

Sure enough, when we compared the list, the previous list had the Ruth contract. He had removed it from the current one. Luckily, the attorney, who was quite pretty, brought Frank's typed list of revisions. It was clear that he had removed the item and that this was no typo.

For years, since Uncle Frank's death, I've been searching for that contract. It's been my white whale. I've heard whispers and chased down rumors. Nothing has ever turned up. Nobody seems to know what happened to it. I began to worry that the Eddie Sloane's Babe

Ruth jersey might be like the contract. Odd that both artifacts involved the same player.

After Rainbow's revelation about Eddie's Phoenix property, I decided to do some research after the game using the computer in the hotel business center. In my hurry to leave Indianapolis, I forgot my laptop. After some digging on the Internet, I learned the property had changed hands several times before its current owners acquired it. Rainbow was right: Eddie did sell it for $1,000,000. I didn't get much further because Ramona interrupted my research.

"How is my baseball man today?"

"Great, I went to a game …" she cut me off.

"I have a surprise for you waiting at my home. My shift is almost over and then we will go to my home for dinner." I tried to protest, honestly. But, she leaned in and suddenly there were entirely too many tongues in my mouth. She then pushed me back in my chair and told me to get dressed for dinner.

"Dressed for dinner?" I looked down at my T-shirt and shorts. "No good?"

"No good. You must have pants. And a shirt with buttons."

"A shirt with buttons? But I …" Cut off mid-sentence with another lean-in. Another kiss. This one left me speechless.

"You get ready now."

I nodded in agreement. In the elevator I tried to remember if I even brought pants and a shirt that buttoned. But the fog of the kiss lifted and I remembered I had brought nice clothes for the upcoming auction. I got dressed quickly, an eager lamb blissfully unaware of the slaughter to come.

I was expecting more illicit hijinks. Instead, we drove to Ramona's family home and I was greeted by her brother opening the front door. He introduced himself and told me he had been expecting me. After shaking his hand, I was welcomed inside where I found a receiving line of brothers, sisters, aunts, cousins, nieces and nephews. It took me twenty minutes of being welcomed before I worked my way up to the parents. The parents! Can you believe that? I've been in town for less than 48 hours! I swore off one-night stands on the spot.

Ramona invited every blood relative in the Mountain Time Zone to meet me and I'm sure there were some non-relatives there as well. I was grilled by someone who I think was a grandmother. At this point, I should point out that my Spanish is not that good. In fact, it's quite awful. So, I'm not sure exactly what I said to her but Grandma pinched my butt a little later in the evening.

Grandma was the least of my worries. Ramona introduced me to her Aunt Sophia, who speaks no English whatsoever. Aunt Sophia asked me if my parents were still alive.

Responding in Spanish, I thought I responded, "Yes, they live in Indianapolis. I don't see them very often, though, they travel a lot."

Aunt Sophia gasped and made the sign of the cross—something she would do the rest of the night whenever she looked at me. Ramona grabbed my arm and pulled me aside.

"How could you say such a thing?"

"What did I say?"

Ramona explained that what I really said was, "Yes, they live in Indianapolis. However, I've yet to drink the blood of the toaster." I should have paid a lot more attention during Spanish classes in college.

By the time I got back to the hotel, I was a wreck. I had been stuffed with food and overwhelmed by Ramona's family. I obviously had made a huge mistake with her, but I had to handle this carefully. As the assistant manager of the hotel, she had access to a lot of my personal information from when I registered. I already had a glance of her temper. I didn't want to see it again. But, what on earth made her think I was ready to meet her family? We had one night! One night. Now there is a Spanish matriarch calling me son and pinching my butt and an aunt who thinks I drink blood from toasters.

This was my fault. I just had to hit on her, didn't I? I told myself I was giving up women. Forever. Or until this trip is over. Or until I find the jersey. Or until tomorrow.

Chapter Six

Jessica gave me the contact information for the auctioneer who sold Eddie's possessions. I was hoping to find something we may have missed. It took me about twenty minutes to get to Scottsdale from my hotel. Avery's Auctions was located in an inconspicuous office complex. It sat at the back end of row after row of identical office suites. A single door with a modest sign was the only clue to the bounty of items within. The property was well maintained and a cactus stood on either side of the doorway. Inside, a receptionist greeted me in a lobby that seemed to have remained untouched since the '80s, aside from regular dusting. The same could be said of the receptionist.

"Hi, I'm inquiring about an auction."

She pointed to a large calendar on the wall without looking up from her magazine and said, "Those are the upcoming auction dates. You can grab one of the corresponding flyers below for details. Go online to see specific item photos and descriptions."

"I was more interested in one that already happened."

She looked up from the magazine, eyes peering over her reading glasses. "Sugar, it's too late to bid on an auction that already took place."

"I don't want to bid, I just wanted to get some information. It was for the auction of Eddie Sloane's items. I believe someone here knew him quite well, and you handled his tax sale. Mr. Boyle is expecting me."

"So, how do you know Eddie?"

"I found his pants."

She looked up from her magazine. "Excuse me?"

"His pants were missing, and I found them for him." I grinned and gave the receptionist a wink.

She shook her head in disgust and called back to the auctioneer. "Mr. Boyle, there is a man here to see you. Says he knows Eddie Sloane and that you're expecting him."

She paused for his reply and I kept smiling at her. "Okay, I'll send him back."

With the warmth of a Marine drill sergeant she pointed to a set of double doors. "I'll buzz you in the first door and then Mr. Boyle's office is the second on the right."

I could tell she didn't know what to make of me, so I pulled out a card before following her instructions. "Thank you so much," I said. I handed her the card and she took it reluctantly. "And if you know anyone who needs help finding their pants, just let me know."

She gasped in disgust and dropped the card. I grinned and walked towards the double doors. Despite her reaction, she pressed the buzzer and the doors opened for me. I made my way to the second door.

"Come in, come in." Larry Boyle put down the meatball sub he was devouring and extended a hand. I shook it and came away with marinara sauce on my hands. I subtly wiped it on the chair when I sat down.

"Welcome, Mr. Quick."

"Just Quick. And thanks for seeing me on such short notice."

"Well, Eddie was a friend. A good man who just had terrible luck. More than once he helped me out of a jam, so if I can return the favor by helping you, I consider it the least I can do. How did you know Eddie?"

"I found his pants."

"Oh?" he was intrigued.

"Eddie wanted his game pants from the 1969 season. I tracked them down."

"Oh, well done! Take you long?"

"About nine months."

"Tenacity, Mr. Quick. That's how you survive in this business. I love an auction filled with people like you. Tenacious collectors and in this case, their hired agents."

"Hired agents?"

"Well, whatever you call yourselves. Doesn't matter. What matters is that your passion for artifacts and memorabilia keeps the auctions going. You're good for business."

"Well, I'm glad to be of help."

"Now, how can I help you?"

"I'm looking for information on the jersey you sold for Eddie."

"Yes, sad business, that jersey. Eddie was hoping his daughter could win that item. It must have been very dear to him. Never seen the man so distraught."

"That's what puzzles me. He had the home jersey, which matched the pants. I helped him find this jersey as well and took care of the framing. So, why would losing this one cause him so much anguish?"

"I seem to recall his daughter asking the same thing."

"Did you take any pictures to promote the sale? Any chance you have a picture of the jersey and frame?"

"I'm certain I do. Give me a minute to look for that auction file on my computer."

As he looked, I continued. "Did you notice anything unusual about the jersey or the frame?"

"Not particularly. I do recall the frame was heavy," Boyle said. "Finely crafted, not the cheap frames people buy at their local arts and craft stores."

"Yes, I had it custom made by a guy I know. He's expensive, but worth every penny."

"Here it is." Boyle turned his monitor towards me so I could see.

"Yes, that's the one." There were three pictures of the jersey and frame. One was straight on, the other two at angles that showed the quality of the frame. It was Eddie's jersey all right—a 1969 Royals road jersey. But I couldn't tell if it was the same frame I had commissioned from George. Something was off. My inner voice was telling me to keep looking.

"I'm getting some glare from the window—can I turn your monitor more?"

"Sure, go ahead."

I adjusted the monitor and stared at the pictures. Without the glare of the sunlight, I could see them in greater detail. Something was off. The frame looked right. The jersey was right. What?

"Royal blue!"

"What?"

"Royal blue. The background fabric for the frame I had made was royal blue. This picture is the light blue they didn't start using until 1973. This isn't the original frame. Or if it is, it's been altered."

"You don't say!"

"I do say. I've got to get a close look at this jersey."

"That might be tricky. I don't suppose you know anything about the man who bought it?"

"Oh, I've heard a few things," I said, purposely vague. "What can you tell me about him?"

"Kind of strange, a wealthy guy like that coming down for one of our auctions. He has such deep pockets you might expect him to show up at Sotheby's. But we're middle of the road. We get mostly thrift store owners, interior designers, collectors and such. He owns real estate, a bat company and whatnot. Men like that don't nickel and dime with grandma's china."

"Jessica thinks he was only there to spite Eddie. He held a grudge on Eddie and wouldn't let it go. He knew that jersey meant a lot to him and he knew it would hurt him to not get it back."

"I know, but to drive him to suicide. It seems like such an over-reaction."

"It's hard to say what you would cling to when you've lost everything. Maybe it was all those memories of younger days."

"But like you said, he had the other '69 jersey. Why would this one mean so much?"

"I don't know, but I guess I need to meet Byrne face to face. Anything else you can tell me about him?"

"Yeah, he's all business and not all that friendly. Don't expect to be welcomed with open arms if he knows you're doing Eddie's daughter a favor."

"Thanks, I'll keep that in mind."

"Good luck, Mr. Quick. I sure liked Eddie. I don't know if it will mean much now that Eddie's gone, but I sure hope you're able to get that jersey back for his daughter."

"I'll keep you posted."

***

Before I could even get the car started to head back to my hotel, I received a call from the police. "Is this Mr. Quick?"

"Yes, can I help you?"

"This is Sergeant Walker with the Scottsdale Police Department."

I had a sick feeling. Nothing good has ever followed the phrase, "This is so-and-so with the police."

"I have a couple of guys here who say you are responsible for them. I can't tell if what they've done today is dementia or vandalism, so I was hoping you could help shed some light on the situation."

"I'm in Scottsdale right now. Tell me where to meet you." He gave me the address and I tracked them down in a posh Scottsdale neighborhood. Tommy and Frank from the Fungo Society were handcuffed on the curb. Their clothes were soaked.

"Do you know these men?"

"I just met them this week."

"They say you're responsible for them."

I looked at them and they shrugged. "We couldn't call our wives," added Tommy.

"What do you know about the Fungo Society,-" the officer continued.

"I know they're a bunch of old ballplayers. Most live here in Arizona year-round or most of the year."

"Did you encourage them to do this?"

"I'm not even sure what it is they've done."

"Do you know why they would want to disrupt Mrs. Byrne's party?"

"Well, they're old. They get confused, I'm sure it wasn't on purpose. If you don't mind my asking, what exactly did they do?"

"The bastard isn't even home!" Frank was yelling.

"Not helping," I responded.

"They drove a convertible into the Byrnes' pool."

"You know how it is with these really old guys. They miss a turn, driving at night, get confused, and then splash. The important thing is, nobody was hurt." I paused and asked, "Nobody was hurt, were they?"

"Nothing serious."

"Probably the worst damage was to Tommy's car, right?"

"It was Mr. Byrne's convertible."

"They all look alike. Honest mistake."

"It's a one-of-a-kind Italian sports car."

"Not an honest mistake?" I asked. The cop shook his head no.

"Any chance you can just give him a ticket?" He shook his head again.

"Should I just follow you to the station?" He nodded yes.

The officer put Tommy and Frank into the back of the police car. I followed them to the station. They questioned me for a while, but I satisfied them that I hadn't put them up to this stunt. Rainbow met me there with his attorney and bailed them out a few hours later. He seemed to think he could get their charges knocked down to misdemeanors with community service as the sentence. I was really glad that Byrne wasn't home or I never would have been able to get a meeting with him.

"What the hell were you guys thinking?"

"We wanted to go in guns blazing!"

"And?"

"And we forgot the guns."

"Thank God, you would have killed someone. You almost did kill someone, according to Sergeant Walker."

"Well, isn't that what you wanted us to do?"

"Me? I don't want revenge on this guy, you do. Besides, if I were in on this I would want you to ruin him. Embarrass him. Not kill him!"

"Oh, that's completely different. Why didn't you say so?" Tommy hit me on the shoulder.

Chapter Seven

My next move was to meet with Byrne. The Fungo Society wanted me to pin a murder on him. Jessica wanted me to buy a jersey from him. I didn't see how I could successfully do both, but paying customers are paying customers. I was pretty certain the Fungos were sending me on a fool's errand, but I figured there must be some way for me to help them gain closure. As for Jessica's job, even if Byrne bought the jersey for spite, I figured greed could beat spite for the right price.

Getting a meeting with Byrne took some finesse. One of the Fungo Society members had a friend of a friend vouch for me to put some distance between us. I didn't even tell him who I was really buying the jersey for, instead claiming it was for a collector in Kansas City.

Byrne world headquarters is something to behold. The seven-story building held a variety of Byrne interests, including real estate, collections, the bat company, and a chain of donut shops. An eclectic mix, but all making money. Or at least that's the impression he and the board of directors wanted you to get when you made a visit to their campus. Seven stories of opulence surrounded by well-manicured grounds. A waterfall beckoned when you turned into the parking lot, a rather conspicuous use of water in a desert. The signs directing you where to park sported the Byrne Bats shamrock logo. The logo also was in the flowerbeds. It was etched in the glass front doors. It was even inlaid into the marble floor of the lobby.

I rode a glass elevator that gave me an excellent view of the lobby shamrock as I ascended to the seventh floor. It struck me that the brand of the bat company was clearly the most important here. Different divisions had different names, but the Byrne Bats brand clearly was front and center.

When the elevator door opened, I had an amazing view of downtown Phoenix before me. Through more glass doors I met a receptionist who sent me to Byrne's administrative assistant. She made me wait about ten minutes before escorting me into Byrne's office. I had tried to make small talk with her, but she wasn't very chatty. As I walked in, I could see Eddie's jersey hanging on the wall facing his desk.

"Good afternoon, Mr. Byrne."

"Have a seat–Mr. Quick is it?" He was all business.

"Yes, you can call me Quick."

"Well Quick, be quick." That joke just won't die. "I understand you have a Red Sox lead for me. Kevin Rose said you wouldn't waste my time. I hope you won't make him out a liar."

"I wouldn't think of wasting your time, but your friend is slightly mistaken. It's a Padres lead I have for you. You are aware that Ted Williams played for the minor league Padres before signing with the Red Sox?"

"I am, go on."

"I have a lead on a Ted Williams jersey from '39. I know you're a collector of Williams-related memorabilia, so I wanted to personally invite you to bid or consider a proxy arrangement."

"I don't use a proxy when it comes to memorabilia. But I do appreciate the offer." He paused and looked me in the eyes. "Seems like something you could have sent me via email. Did you have to come here in person to get shot down?" Obviously, the man is a jerk. But I had to tread lightly, because the Williams jersey was just a smokescreen.

"No," I replied, "I understand you have an item that is of interest to one of my clients."

"Really, and what do you know about my collection?"

"It's my business to know. To put people in contact with each other whose interests might align."

"All so you can make a meager living off the commission."

I began to wonder if he did this to everybody. "I suppose you could say that."

"I just did. You make deals that allow you to catch a spring training game once in a while or maybe buy an autographed baseball from your favorite player. I make deals that allow me to buy entire teams."

"You're buying a baseball team?"

"Minor league, and of course I can't disclose the details to you. I'm projecting a monster year after my new bats hit the shelves. And this particular team is ripe for a buyout. Of course, you didn't hear that from me and I would deny it if you did."

I was starting to hate this guy with every particle of my being. He pointed to a framed Randy Johnson jersey. "Notice the frame that jersey is in? Go ahead, take a look."

I looked at the jersey first, quietly assessing its authenticity in my mind. It was made by Rawlings and had the 2002 All-Star Patch on the sleeve. Although Johnson made the All-Star team that year, he didn't appear in the game. So, the jersey had minimal wear, save for a few telltale tobacco stains. I decided it was legit. Probably would fetch around $4,500 at auction. Then I studied the frame; it was fairly well made, but mass produced. Etched in the glass in the lower right corner was the Byrne Bats logo. It seemed thicker than most jersey cases. "We're moving thousands of these per week," he bragged.

I doubted that. The high-end jersey market didn't seem large enough for him to be selling thousands of deluxe frames, but I didn't want to argue. "Congratulations. In the meantime, I would like to know if you would be interested in selling that 1969 Royals jersey you bought at auction a while back."

"Eddie's jersey. No, I don't think so."

I got up from my chair and walked over to the jersey to study it. "It's not a particularly valuable jersey," I said over my shoulder. "Game used and authentic, but come on, it's only Eddie Sloane. A middling infielder on a pretty lousy team?"

"Mr. Quick, it obviously has value or you wouldn't be sitting here. It isn't that daughter of his who put you up to this, is it?"

"My buyer is in Kansas City. He's opening a new establishment and is looking for Royals memorabilia to dress it out. A 1969 jersey would help round out his collection." The background fabric was indeed the powder blue I had noticed in the photo at the auctioneer's, not the royal blue it had been when I sold it to Eddie. Something else looked strange about it as well, but I was hesitant to stare too long and give anything away.

"What kind of establishment?"

"It's a microbrewery and restaurant called Tap 69 in honor of the year the Royals joined the league."

"My trophy in a bar? Get the hell out of my office."

"He's willing to pay for it. Much more than you did."

"It has sentimental value."

"Why?"

"Maybe you haven't heard. The old man showed me up. I can't have that in my business."

I got up to leave, determined to help the Fungo Society get revenge. But there was something about that Royals jersey that didn't seem right. I also noticed another jersey in a frame that was angled against the back wall of the office. There were boxes in front of it, so I couldn't see what jersey it was.

"There's only one thing I would trade for it," Byrne said.

"What's that?"

"Moonlight Graham."

"You want a movie prop?"

"No, Mr. Quick. The real Moonlight Graham. Get me something, anything from the real-life Archibald 'Moonlight' Graham and I will trade you for the Sloane jersey."

My heart sunk.

"You can't be serious. The value of an authentic Moonlight Graham artifact would be much higher than Eddie's jersey. How is that a fair trade?"

"Who said anything about fair? I know what you want. You know what I want. I think that concludes our business for today."

I studied him and Eddie's jersey for a moment longer. He buzzed his assistant to show me out.

Shit! I knew this would be a challenge. I called Kevin and told him to start sniffing.

***

I managed to avoid Ramona when I got back to the hotel and went to bed early. The next morning it was breakfast with the Fungo Society in a private room at Denny's. I let them know about my experience with the jersey, but I didn't mention the fabric. I was still trying to come up with the reason why it was changed. It seemed like an odd thing for Eddie to do and it had to be him. His daughter didn't know anything about it and the auctioneer's photo confirmed it had been changed prior to the auction.

The guys were particularly fired up that morning because of Tommy and Frank's pool escapade. Now they wanted to top it.

"We could burn one of his buildings down," yelled Hal as I walked in.

"Too illegal! We don't want to go to jail." Rainbow looked at Tommy.

"Says in the paper he's getting an award next week. We could go to the banquet and disrupt it."

"Anyone going to this?" I asked. Nobody said yes. "You need a way to get in or get invited. But are you sure this is how you want to do it? It seems pretty small. How about something more permanent and less likely to get you sent to jail?"

"Well, Mr. Genius, what do you have in mind?"

"I don't know, I'm just trying to keep you guys out of jail."

"Ah, you don't know shit. We've raised all kinds of hell and managed to keep ourselves out of jail," said Hal.

"Yeah, well a lot of people covered for you back in the day. You're not the celebrities you were back then," I reminded them.

"Oh, yeah smart-ass? Well, you were never a celebrity, so there."

"No, I wasn't." I saw a chance to distract them from doing something stupid. "Tell me what it was like being a ballplayer in the '70s."

Rainbow leaned back in his chair, crossed his hands behind his chair and reminisced, "It was the best. But it was a turbulent time. Free agency was something we never dreamed of when we were coming up in the minors. Then suddenly Curt Flood happened and we started to see guys making real money. Of course, nothing like the crazy amounts they are paying now. But every new free agent contract was a 'wow' moment. Catfish Hunter, Reggie Jackson, Tom Seaver. The contracts those guys got were beyond our wildest dreams. Of course nobody in this room ever got that kind of money."

"It wasn't about the money for me. Hell, I would have played for free and sometimes it felt like I was." Rainbow laughed. "But we had the time of our lives. Playing in all those ballparks, traveling, meeting new people. I wouldn't trade it for the world."

"It was about money for me after my wife got pregnant with our third child. That's why I didn't stick around with you guys in Kansas City."

"Yeah, and Eddie didn't let you forget that the rest of the guys were pissed that you left." They all laughed.

"What did he do?" I asked.

"He let go of his bat when we played them in spring training. Made like it slipped out of his hand, but we knew it was on purpose. The bat sailed right over his head and landed almost at second base."

"Did he get ejected?"

"No, he managed to talk his way out of it, but Ronnie Cox, the Indians manager, was steamed. He almost got ejected trying to argue that Eddie should be ejected."

"Yeah, but he didn't hold onto to the grudge much after that."

They all got silent and I was afraid to ask why. Still I mustered up the courage. "Why's that?"

"My wife was pregnant and we lost the baby. Eddie and his wife were pretty good to us. Helped us get through that March. They treated us like we were still part of the family. Don't know how I could have made it through it without them."

The Prophet added, "Yep, Eddie was a great man. Not a great ballplayer, but a great man." They all chuckled a bit. But I could tell that to a man, they were thinking back to some part that Eddie had played in their lives. That's when the anger came back.

"We should do something."

"Yeah, what the hell are we doing sitting here jawing when that bastard is still out there?"

"We should go burn his house down. Who's with me?" Tommy made for the door and I grabbed him by the arm. He weighed all of a buck forty-five, so he wasn't all that hard to restrain.

"You are not going to burn the guy's house down."

"Why not?"

"For one, you're too old and too slow to do it without getting caught." I didn't get the second reason out of my mouth. Tommy hit me in the head with his cane and went out the door. I didn't follow him because my second reason was that he didn't have a license or a car anymore. Nobody had followed him outside.

Hal woke up from his nap. "Where did Tommy go?"

"To burn down Byrne's house."

"You don't say. I'd kinda like to see that."

"Really, so you could go to jail with him?"

"No," he stopped and laughed. "I would like to see that old man with the shakes try to light the match." The room erupted with laughter.

Chapter Eight

Later that afternoon, I was staring off into space, contemplating exactly nothing while listening to ESPN go on about this free agent and that one. I was in a fog, quietly sipping my whiskey, when I heard someone burst through the door behind me. I didn't turn around to see who or what it was like the rest of the bar. I knew it was Rainbow.

"Quick, I've got big news. Huge!"

"Hi Rainbow." I turned to face him and noticed several of the Fungo Society members streaming in behind him. They surrounded me at the bar as Rainbow continued.

"Byrne is making a huge product announcement at the Phoenix Memorabilia Show Saturday."

"Yeah, so?"

"So, that's where we could get our revenge. And you could help us."

"Me?"

"Yes, you. You will have access around the show. You can get us inside."

"It's open to the public. You don't need me to get you inside. Unless you're too cheap to pay the $10 ticket price."

"But you could let us go behind the scenes so we can nail the bastard," Hal chimed in.

I asked, "Just what do you have in mind?"

"We were thinking you could help us come up with that."

"You want me to get you behind the scenes and you don't even know what you want to do?"

"Nail the bastard. That's what we want to do," yelled Hal.

I looked at Hal and rolled my eyes. "What does that mean, Hal? How do you want to nail him? Do you want to disrupt the presentation? Do you want to set off smoke bombs, cause a ruckus and get yourselves arrested? Do you want to bring in a bunch of strippers to get up on stage right when he's making his big announcement to make him look sexist? What? What do you think you're going to do?"

"That's a hell of an idea!"

"What is?"

"All of it!"

"I knew there had to be a reason you hired this guy, Rainbow." Teddy gave me a pat on the back and got up. All the guys started moving towards the door.

"Well done, son. Well done," said Hank.

"Wait, I was being sarcastic. I didn't mean for you to do any of that stuff."

"Great plan kid," exclaimed another Fungo as he passed.

"Love the idea!" said another.

Holy crap! What did I just do? I didn't mean to imply they should do any of that stuff. Could I be viewed as an accomplice when they inevitably get arrested? I finished my whiskey and ordered another.

Ah, what did I have to worry about? These guys forget where they've put their keys twice a day. They all will take naps and forget the whole thing in a few hours, I tried to convince myself. Of course, I was wrong.

***

The Phoenix Memorabilia Show draws about 15,000 visitors over three days. There are bigger shows, but this one had some flair because of its proximity to spring training and the lineup of players and former players making appearances. All that autograph signing keeps the turnstiles moving.

For this show, at least one current and former player from each of the MLB teams represented in the Cactus League would be making an appearance sometime during the weekend. They were scheduled each hour and lines could be pretty long to get a baseball, picture or baseball card signed. The marquee players were signing on Saturday, the day with the highest expected turnout. This also was the day that Byrne Bats would be making its surprise announcement.

I promised the guys I would send along any news I could uncover about Byrne's big reveal. So far, none of the insiders I knew could tell me anything of value. Byrne was playing this one close to the vest.

This convention had me concerned. I had several items that clients wanted me to track down. Occasionally, clients will have me act as their agent. They give me their top dollar amount and have me bid on items they want. I get a commission, plus a bonus if I can get the item significantly under budget. This show featured a memorabilia auction that promised some rarely seen sports artifacts. It was critical for me to be there in order to bid on three items. One was a Lou Gehrig game-used jersey. It had been in a private collection for many years and as part of an estate liquidation it was coming to auction. Item two was a Stan Musial jersey from his minor league seasons with Williamson. I didn't expect this jersey to go for near the amount of the Gehrig jersey, and since this auction was in Phoenix and not St. Louis or even near Jupiter, Florida, where the Cardinals play their spring training games, the likelihood that a huge number of Cardinal fans would be there was low. In fact, I was skeptical about the authenticity of the jersey, given the odd location of the auction, so I planned to proceed with great caution.

The final item was intriguing: A set of four seats reportedly from Shibe Park in Philadelphia where the Athletics used to play. The buyer was in Devon, Pennsylvania. I wanted to win the auction for the commission. But I wasn't thrilled about how I was going to get the seats from the convention hall to a UPS or FedEx store to ship. My rental car was a Honda Fit, courtesy of the Fungo Society. It was as slow and as small as the plastic toy car I bought my nephew Elliot for Christmas.

My other great worry was the nature of the diabolical plan of the Fungo Society. I didn't want to get lumped into whatever it was they were going to do (especially if it turned out to be what I had recklessly suggested in the bar). I couldn't let their shenanigans distract me from buying these three items. I had bills to pay.

Normally, I do a lot of research before going to an auction. I make calls, do Internet research, and talk with other dealers. Sometimes it might necessitate travel to a relevant library or the Baseball Hall of Fame if the item is of particular historical significance and the payoff is going to be huge. However, for this bit of research, I decided to go to the American Legion Post #107.

Donnie Bird is a dealer in Phoenix. He's a transplanted St. Louis native who moved to the southwest to make his wife happy. Bird is not his last name, but a nickname he got as a huge Cardinals fan and an expert on Cardinals collectibles. If anything of significance related to the Cardinals moves, Donnie Bird knows about it. Donnie was managing a small-time card show in advance of the big event.

The backroom of the American Legion hall was a cross section of collecting humanity. There were middle class dads dressed in tracksuits, sometimes with a teenager in tow looking for one of the shiny new card releases. Old men, shabbily dressed and days removed from their last shower, parked in front of boxes with rows and rows of cards. They would be there for the next few hours sorting through box after box with a checklist, trying to complete sets.

I had several observations about the dealers. First, many of them are collecting, too. I would say 85 percent probably bought as much as they sold. They would leave their own tables for 10 to 15 minutes at a time looking through cards at some other dealer's table. Secondly, all the dealers seemed to be struggling. The market isn't what it used to be, they would say. "Tough to get top dollar in this market," one complained. "Everybody wants something for nothing."

The dealers would complain about customers nickel and diming them, but then would turn around and do the same thing to their fellow dealers when they wanted to buy something.

It was a culture all unto itself. Another thing I noticed was how one particular type of kid would lighten the moods and the hearts of the older dealers. Older dealers don't mind selling the new stuff, but it lacks the romance of the old cards. This is understandable and not much of a mystery. Every generation thinks its music, its literature, its sports heroes were better than the ones before and after. It's human nature. It's the same with sports cards. In some ways, I suppose they are right.

The card industry went through a period when the market was saturated with product. One of the reasons the older stuff is so valuable isn't just because the players were somehow better, but because so few of the cards actually are around today. Prior to the 1980s, collecting was disorganized. There were no card protectors, no authenticating services, no monthly printed price guides.

In other words, fewer older cards were printed, fewer survived kids putting them in the spokes of their bicycles, and even fewer exist in pristine condition (especially since they were packed with gum until the '90s). After market saturation, the card companies went the other way with intentional short run and high-end product. Although this meant the product was more rare, and thus more valuable, it also meant that cards were being sold at such high prices kids couldn't afford to buy them.

Cards that once cost 50 cents per pack will now set you back anywhere from a couple dollars to over five dollars per pack. It's a double-edged sword. The companies have eliminated the price point where casual buyers won't destroy their own cards, as with bicycles. This was because there were no casual buyers anymore. Now, only those serious about collecting and protecting their cards could afford to do it. But by eliminating the casual buyer, they cut out a generation of card collecting kids. Kids who collected for the love of it. Kids who may not even love it yet, but might buy a few cards and get hooked. And if they never get hooked as kids, they don't come back to the hobby as adults. Which, ironically, is the arc of a large portion of collectors. They collect as kids. Give it up during their high school/college I'm-too-cool-for-this phase. Then when they have kids, that passion starts to come back. The fewer kids who start, the fewer there are to come back when they become adults.

And that's why one kid captured the hearts of many of the old dealers. A twelve-year-old named Simon was looking for Cardinals of the 1960s and I thought Donnie Bird was going to adopt him as his own grandson on the spot. Donnie pulled up a chair for the boy and allowed him to carefully sort through his boxes. Most kids, he wouldn't let them touch his well-preserved cards of the '60s, but this kid took great care.

The dealers on either side of Donnie drew near to what I can only imagine was in their world like seeing a Sasquatch—a kid who wanted '60s baseball cards. It's not like dealers don't like other kids. It's just that most of them show up with the Derek Jeter they got in a pack of cards and want the dealer to buy it off them for the appraised price in publications like Beckett magazine. Kids don't get that the dealer has to be able to buy for a lower price and then mark up the card and make a profit in order to eat and have electricity. No kid gets this. They just know Beckett says the card is worth $30 and why the hell won't the dealer give them $30.

Dealers survive by the business of the speculators— the ones who plan to sell all their cards someday in the near future for what they believe will be a fortune. But they are energized by a true collector. True collectors are excited by the value of their cards, looking for a deal just like the rest. But while true collectors might talk of selling their cards someday, the dealers know that day is the day after those true collectors die. They never get around to it. They simply can't part with their prized possessions.

"Donnie, what do you know about the Musial minor league jersey up for auction next Saturday?"

"Phoenix show?"

"Yeah, that's the one."

"Owned by a collector in Scottsdale, supposedly."

"I know what the auction catalog says. I want to know if you think it's legit. Or if you've seen it with your own eyes."

"Oh, yeah I've seen it. It's legit."

"Really? I was skeptical because they are auctioning it here. Seems like the kind of thing you would try to move in St. Louis."

"The guy who owned it got taken by a local dealer. He's just trying to unload it quickly and under the radar so he can cash in and move on."

"Well, this auction is hardly under the radar."

"Actually, it is kind of is under the radar, despite being in the previous owner's backyard."

"How so?"

"The local media isn't going to cover this in depth. Just a superficial 'we're here at the show' kind of thing.

The previous owner won't be attending, so he flips it quick."

"If he wanted to flip it quick, why not put it on eBay?"

"Word is, Carlos Gomez is going to be there."

"Who is he?

"Have you heard of CG Frames & Displays?"

"Yes, they're the ones that make those display cases for bats, balls, cards, etc. Correct?"

"That's right. Word is he's involved with some big promotion that Byrne Bats is doing."

"Byrne said he was launching a new line of jersey frames. I bet Gomez is manufacturing them and Byrne is private labeling them. I think he's going to lose a bunch of money on them."

"What makes you say that?"

"He told me he was moving thousands per week. It's seems like too high end of an item to move that many per week. Anyway, back to the auction. Do you think the seller knew this and put the Musial jersey in to get Gomez to bid?"

"Absolutely. I would bet the World Series trophy that he will have a shell bidder going against Gomez to drive up the price."

"How much do you think it could go for?"

"Gomez could go as high as fifteen or sixteen thousand."

"Fifteen thousand? Damn!

"Why, were you thinking of making a run at it?"

"Yeah, I've got a client who wants it, but they aren't going to go that high. You really think it will go that high?"

"I said could, not would. Doesn't mean he will spend that much. And it's not a major league jersey—some people put much more stock in that. However, Musial's jersey from his days playing for the Navy in WWII went for $16,000 about a year ago."

"Looks like I might be shut out on this one, but thanks for the help." I nodded towards the kid. "What's he looking for?"

"Sixty-four Cardinals team set."

"No kidding?"

"Yeah, isn't it great?"

"Tell you what," I handed him a twenty. "Put twenty on the kid's account for helping me out."

"Will do! Good luck with the auction."

As I walked out I noticed the mirror ball in the center of the room started to spin. I wondered how long it had been there—was it a '70s original? I also wondered if the ceiling tiles had ever been changed since the '70s. Mostly I wondered how I was going to outbid Gomez for the Musial jersey.

***

I got to the convention early on Saturday. My pass let me in the hall long before the general public was allowed in. It gave me a chance to talk with various dealers and card vendors, and get a sense of the layout. There was a main hall where the auction would take place. A stage was set up on the back wall with a small food court to the left and a curtained-off hospitality area on the right. The stage, the food court, and the hospitality area took up about one-fourth of the room. The other three quarters was populated with rows of vendor booths.

These vendors ranged from card brands and collectible manufacturers to high-end memorabilia dealers and large-volume sports auction houses.

Adjacent to the main hall was a side room with another 75 booths devoted to new and used trading card dealers. It was like a mini-Comic Con for sports nerds. And I was one of the sports nerdiest. One tactic I noticed about this show that was different from other conventions was the use of booth babes. This is the controversial practice of hiring attractive women to work the booths and attract potential customers. Detractors say it's sexist. Supporters say it boosts sales. I say capitalism is great, especially when capitalism is wearing heels.

At the Maxwell Auctions booth, I found a high-heeled capitalist and tried to press her for information. Unfortunately, she didn't seem to want to turn on the charm until the show actually opened. I wondered if the booth babes had a union because she had no intention of engaging in flirtatious behavior until 9 a.m. Her co-worker, a male capitalist in loafers, however, sniffed me out for a buyer.

"Hey, I appreciate that you're going to be bidding on some of our items today, but we can't give you any info that gives you an advantage over other bidders."

"I wouldn't think of it." I was lying, of course. "I just wanted to know if I could get a look at that Musial jersey. I have some concerns about the authenticity."

"We'll be putting out all the items for inspection one hour before the auction. You're welcome to check us out then and have all your questions answered."

"Okay, suit yourself." I said. "But it would be a shame to put it out and then find out it's a fake." I started to walk away and he grabbed my arm. The booth babe suddenly seemed interested.

"Just out of curiosity, what makes you think it's a fake?"

"I watched Musial sign a 1940 jersey just like it and it's hanging in the St. Louis Children's Hospital. Hard for me to believe there are two of these floating around. It's possible. Just not likely."

"And why should I believe you, mister ..." He looked down to see the name on my badge. "Mr. Quick." He paused as if trying to access some long-forgotten nugget of information tucked away in a rarely dusted corner of his brain. "Quick...," he trailed off. "Quick! You're Jonathan Quick?"

"Call me Quick."

"I thought you would be older."

"I get that a lot."

He looked at the booth babe. "Mr. Quick has a reputation as an expert on vintage jerseys and other relics."

She smiled and nodded. "And a reputation for…"— Mr. Loafers seemed to have just accessed another nugget from that corner—"a reputation for…" His eyes widened and he stepped in between me and the booth babe. "Other things," he finally said.

"Would you like me to verify it?"

"Yes, that would be a good idea." He looked back over his shoulder and said to the booth babe, "I'll be right back."

I smiled at her and she smiled with a bit of curiosity about the "other things." He grabbed my arm and pulled me along. "Let's go."

***

"I have two Williamson jerseys. One is from the local source here in Arizona and one is from a Stan Musial lot we acquired last year. We sold the other items from the lot but we know one of the jerseys to be a fake."

"Oh, why's that?"

"I'll show you in a minute." Here's the locally sourced one."

I started with the tag. The manufacturer was Spalding. That was correct for the period, 1939. The wool seemed to have the right feel. Weathered and worn. There were hints of headfirst dives for a ground ball. A faint grass stain for good measure. The jersey number was correct. "It's legit. My fears were that it was fake since the seller wasn't trying to move it in St. Louis where it would fetch a better price."

"I would appreciate your discretion in not pointing that out to our seller if he happens to attend. And I do thank you for the once-over. I'm new to this and I was trying to make a splash and impress my boss."

"Happy to help. And maybe you can do me a favor someday as well. By the way, what about the other Williamson jersey?"

"Oh, yeah. I have it over here. There was a telltale sign inside: The name Williamson Colts on the inner neck. I figure it had to be some semi-pro team that the owner of the other Musial items was duped into buying. Seems strange he would have fallen for it."

My heart skipped a beat. I didn't let on, but replied, "I would still like to see it."

He reached into a large crate and pulled out a box with a framed jersey. He opened the lid so I could inspect it. "I'm not sure what to do with it. We've made good money from the rest, so it's not a question of not turning a profit. I just don't know how to position it."

I ignored his babbling for a good five minutes and studied every inch of it. This was a 1938 Williamson jersey with Stan Musial's number on the back. They were convinced it wasn't an actual Musial because the word "Colts" was embroidered on the neck. "Remember that favor?"

"Yes?"

"I'm cashing it in now. I know a bar owner in West Virginia near Williamson who would love to have this. I'll give you $200 bucks for it."

"Mr. Quick, I don't know."

"Look, you're certain it's not an actual Musial jersey. You can't put it in that auction." I pointed to all the stuff they were going to list. "I take it off your hands and you have one less thing to take back to Chicago."

"Alright, it's yours."

I was so glad he didn't ask me the one question that would have killed the deal. Notice I said, "you're certain." I didn't say I was certain. In fact I was certain that it was an authentic Stan Musial jersey! The Williamson Red Birds were known as the Colts their first two seasons of existence, 1937 and 1938. Was it authenticated by these newbies? No, but it was authenticated by me and that was all that mattered. I knew it wasn't a fake—I've seen too many of those to know the difference. It was the right material, right era, right name, and right number. If Musial's Navy jersey fetched $16,000, this could land in that neighborhood too.

It also meant that I didn't need to worry about bidding against Gomez. My client would be happier with this jersey and my cut would be much higher. Suddenly, I felt invincible. When I returned to the auditorium, the booth babe was already working her magic on some guys from Tempe. They didn't look like buyers to me. But 10 minutes with her, and these guys would be over at the ATM transferring money or getting cash so they could bid on some autographed baseball that she batted her eyes and said would be so "hot" to own. Whatever they were paying her today, they definitely were going to earn it back.

I decided to find Rainbow and see if I could talk them out of whatever nonsense the Fungos were going to try.

Chapter Nine

I found Rainbow sitting alone in the food court. He was sipping a coffee and calmly surveying the scene. He was too calm for my taste. Either they were overconfident about whatever they were going to pull or they had decided against it. I was hoping for the latter. "Morning, Rainbow."

"Quick. You on the job today or are you planning to help us?"

"I'm working today, but I was hoping you guys had given up on this nonsense."

"Us, give up? No way! We're on a mission. You wouldn't believe what we have planned for this guy. Let me tell you how it's going to go down."

"No, maybe you better not. That way, later I can deny I knew anything about it."

"Okay, suit yourself. But make sure you're in the main hall when the press conference happens. You're not going to want to miss this."

"I'll be here. I've got to go see a man about a jersey."

Ruben pointed to the restrooms. "Over there, Quick."

"No, that wasn't a euphemism. I really am going to see a man about a jersey."

"A-you-fa what?"

"Never mind. I'll see you later."

Wilbur Thomas is an expert in Babe Ruth relics and memorabilia. He is as old as dirt, but still sharp as a tack. Semi-retired now, Wilbur was always in demand at shows like this. Dealers would have him authenticate a Ruth item and entertain potential buyers with stories of Ruth finds through the years. I had called Wilbur the night before and set up a meeting at the Zander Auction booth. The Zander folks had piles of money, so the booth was decked out with wood and marble. Even the booth babes were dressed classier than the others with little black dresses and lots of pearls. They even had Wilbur in a tuxedo, which made me laugh out loud.

"Wilbur! I didn't think I would see you in a tux until you were dead."

"Yeah, well I'll probably outlive you, smart ass."

"Probably, you're not as reckless as I am."

"I look pretty good don't I?"

"Yes, you do," I replied.

"Thinking of asking one of those ladies over there out on a date after this show is over."

"Really? Wilbur, your taste in women is getting better."

"Yeah, well you know what happened to my last wife."

"Actually, I don't. I think it's been about five years since the last time I saw you. She didn't pass away?" Suddenly I felt really bad.

"No, she ran off with an investment banker. Can you believe that?"

"You don't say? I'm shocked."

"Quick, you can't BS me. I've known you too long. Remember when you tried to pull that fake Ruth on me in Atlantic City?"

"That's not fair. I didn't know that was a fake. That's why I brought it to you. I can't believe you're still sore about that."

"I saw right through you. You were nervous and acting weird. I didn't even have to look at it to tell it was fake."

"You're forgetting things, old man. I told you that the seller was a mob boss. I had a hunch it might be fake, I'll give you that. But do you think I wanted to be the guy to tell him that it wasn't worth anything and somebody had taken him for a ride? Hell no! At least by me bringing it to you, a nationally known expert would be the word. If the people who were lower on the food chain didn't realize it was a fake—like me—then he might feel a little less angry about being swindled by whoever sold him the jersey."

"How did you get messed up with a guy like that anyway?"

"There was a girl..."

He raised his hands and brushed me off. "Ah, there's always a girl in your stories. You're going to get yourself killed over a girl someday, Quick. Settle down."

One of the booth babes walked by and I followed her with my eyes. "Not a bad idea, Wilbur."

"Ahhhh," he grunted and started to walk away. I caught him by the arm.

"Hold on, I really need to ask you some questions. There is a Ruth jersey I want to know about."

"Alright, let's go have a seat." He parted the curtain in the back of the display and we walked into a small hospitality area exclusive to the Zander employees and VIP guests. A very well-dressed man was sitting at a round table with another gentleman who obviously was a customer. One of the booth babes picked up the bat they had been studying and replaced it in a storage case. She bent down to retrieve another smaller case and the customer couldn't take his eyes off her. The salesman looked up and smiled at us as if he knew this customer was his for the taking. And you thought sex appeal only sold cars and Hardee's Thickburgers.

I sat down with Wilbur at a table a little removed from the salesman and his prey. "So, what do you know about Babe Ruth Dodgers jerseys?"

"Jerseys? I doubt there are plural. Unless you're talking home and road. The road has never turned up. Is that the one you think you've found?"

"No, no. Maybe I didn't explain it well on the phone. I'm looking for the home jersey."

"Eddie Sloane's?"

"You knew Eddie had it?"

Wilbur reached over and slapped the side of my head. "Boy, what the hell's the matter with you? I know everything about everything Babe Ruth. Of course I knew Eddie had it."

"Then where is it now? That's why I'm here."

"That, I don't know."

I stared at him and considered the irony. "You just told me..."

"I know what I just told you but I'm telling you, I don't know where Eddie's Ruth jersey is. Are you sure he sold it to Bruce Bailey at KC Collectibles all those years ago? Because I have my doubts."

"His daughter has a receipt. Why do you suspect he didn't sell it?"

"Remember when Bailey went bankrupt in the 2008 crash?"

"Yeah, I remember. Everyone was hurting that year."

"Well I had a friend get me a copy of the asset list because it's public information. The jersey wasn't on it. Now remember, this guy swindled a hell of a lot of people and owed a lot of taxes. So the IRS went over his assets with a fine-tooth comb. That jersey wasn't there."

"Any chance he sold it?"

"Not a chance. That jersey was too big of a deal. To unload it and get anything close to value for it, he would have had to have brought it to auction. It's not likely that anyone in his circle would have bought it.

The Feds were looking at everybody he ever spoke to, so people were keeping a distance. You've been in this business long enough to know that the really big ticket items are bought by people who want to the world to know that they own the trophy. So, I highly doubt that even if it was sold secretly that word wouldn't leak out eventually."

"So you think Bailey has it hidden away somewhere?"

"Unless Eddie lied about selling it in the first place," Wilbur said.

"Like I said, his daughter has the receipt. I haven't seen the receipt in person, but I can take a look."

"Quick, why are you looking into this? Do you have a buyer?"

"No, I just have a hunch."

"Yeah, what's that?"

"I think one of Eddie's business partners might have it."

"Really, who?"

"Carl Byrne."

"What makes you think that?"

"It doesn't make sense that Eddie took his life over a jersey that nobody would pay a fortune over. But imagine if someone conned you out of all your money and you found out they also had the very valuable item you sold in the first place?"

"I'm not following you," Wilbur said.

"My hunch is that Byrne bought the Ruth jersey from KC Collectibles after Eddie embarrassed him just to rub his face in it. Think about it. Byrne gambled and lost all of Eddie's money and still winds up with the Ruth jersey. Then he goes to Eddie's bankruptcy auction and acquires his Royals jersey out from under him. Now, Eddie has no money, no valuable assets, and not even his own jersey."

"That's pretty thin. It's an okay theory, but I don't know if I buy it. Any chance the daughter kept it and is keeping it quiet?"

"No, I don't think so. She seemed not to be aware of it until I brought it up."

His glasses had slid down his nose, and he looked at me directly over the top of the frames. "You've been fooled by a woman before."

"Seriously, are you going to bring that up again?"

"I'm just saying, she might not be all that she seems." He started laughing. "You nearly ruined your reputation on that one, boy!"

I hated this story. But I knew what was coming. Whenever he thought I was being too full of myself, he brought up Kandy with a K. I fell hard for Kandy with a K (as opposed to with a C). Now before your mind starts going there, no, she was not a stripper as the name might imply. I daresay a stripper would have been far less devious. Kandy with a K was an associate of a rival dealer. This dealer happened to know I was in the possession of a baseball signed by the '61 Yankees. I gave—not sold—the ball to this woman whose father supposedly was a lifelong Yankee fan and battling cancer.

After she went back East to share the ball with daddy, she stopped taking my calls. Turns out Daddy wasn't a retired cop in Brooklyn. The man who named Kandy with a K was a plastic surgeon in Dallas and Kandy's employer listed the ball in an auction a month later. I was young and foolish, and well, you get the idea.

"You gave a girl named Kandy with a K the baseball of a lifetime. And she handed it over to Empire Auctions who made a killing on it." He laughed for a good five minutes.

"Did you ever see her again?"

"Nope," I answered with malice.

"Was it worth it?"

I thought about it for a moment. He hit me. "No, I suppose not."

"You're still smitten by her, aren't you?"

"Let's change the subject," I suggested.

"You're sure Eddie's daughter is being level with you, then."

I wasn't about to tell him that there was a discrepancy in the price she told me the land sold for versus what Rainbow told me. I would never hear the end of it. "I think so. There is no logical reason I can think of why she would lie about it. If she had it, she would want to sell it. If Byrne or someone else has it we're at a dead end."

"Well if that possibility is eliminated, we have to consider that maybe Eddie hid the jersey and didn't get around to telling his daughter or anyone else where. That receipt could be fake."

"I thought about that, but why wouldn't he have brought it out of hiding when his finances went south? I'm pretty sure he could have made himself whole if he had been able to sell it."

"Maybe it was stolen," Wilbur said.

"Again, someone would try to unload it and to get the kind of money it's worth, you've got to take it to auction. You just don't walk into a pawn shop with that jersey."

"Any chance it was in the auction and it was missed?"

"What do you mean?"

"Like hidden is some piece of furniture?"

"I don't think so," I sighed. "Remember, Eddie was still alive when his auction happened. He would have kept the jersey out of it. There's no way he would have risked putting in there."

"Then it's still in the stuff he has."

"I suppose. I'll talk to his daughter and see if we can go through all of his possessions again."

The salesman rose up and nearly shouted, "Well thank you, Mr. Banks!" Apparently Mr. Banks had made a big purchase. And the booth babe seemed very impressed with his big purchase because she took his arm and walked him out of the hospitality area.

Wilbur stood up. "Good luck, Quick. Keep me posted. If I hear of anything coming to auction, I'll let you know."

"Thanks, Wilbur."

"If it does come up for sale somewhere, what are you going to do?"

"Not much I can do, I guess. I don't think anyone can prove it's been stolen or any crime has taken place. It's just curious. It's a mystery. You know me, I don't like unanswered questions."

I left Wilbur to flirt with booth babes less than half his age. Now I needed to have a look at the other items I needed for my customers. It was almost 11 a.m., and the auctioneers were placing the merchandise out for inspection. Bidders were getting their numbers and passes to get in to the auction area. My all-access pass got me in, but I needed a bidding number, so I had to wait in line. This was an interesting group of humanity. Not the same crowd as at the baseball card meet. These people were dressed more for business—no sweat pants or mesh-back hats. Some of the men had wives, girlfriends and/or mistresses. Hard to tell which. These women were fashionably dressed. The card-show girlfriends mostly wore tight jeans with a pack of smokes in one back pocket and a cell phone in the other.

There was a combination of dealers, agents, and high-end collectors. After about ten minutes I got my bidding bracelet and number.

Chapter Ten

I went to check out the seats from Shibe Park first. Everyone would be making a beeline for the Gehrig jersey first and I didn't want to fight that crowd. Besides, I didn't want to tip off anyone who might be lurking about to see who the bidding competition might be. The pregame, as I like to call it, is every bit as important as the actual auction. There are a lot of regulars at these things and we're always trying to outdo and outthink each other. You don't want to let people know how many items you're looking at because it might tip someone off to how much you can actually spend. This can work against you when that knowledge is out there. A shifty dealer will drive you up on something he or she doesn't necessarily want in order to drive down your ability to bid against them on an item they really want. We're a ruthless lot. I also knew that there would be lots of non-dealers just there to get a glimpse of the Gehrig jersey. Once they cleared out, I would casually have a look.

In the meantime, the stadium seats were my focus. Shibe Park stood in Philadelphia from 1909 to 1976. It was the home of the Phillies and the Athletics originally and was the first steel and concrete constructed baseball stadium. Ben Shibe, the Athletics' co-owner at the time, said it was for the "masses and the classes." Often compared to a church or a government courthouse, it had an unusually formal design with a domed tower and signature cupola at the top. Construction began in April 1908 and Shibe Park was ready for the 1909 season.

These seats were not restored, which in this case was good. Unless you have a good history and documentation, anyone might be able to pass off a restored seat as coming from whatever stadium. Usually fakes are easily spotted when forgers try to attach some stadium name or logo that wasn't actually there back in the day. I really wasn't expecting these to be fake—too public and too many serious collectors in the house. Try to pass off bad merchandise in this crowd and you'll never host an auction again. Word gets around fast in our circle.

My hope was that they looked beat up enough to be vintage but not so bad that my client would be embarrassed to display them. It's a fine line to walk. The client was from a small town outside Philadelphia. An eye surgeon, he had made a pile of cash as both a surgeon and owner of a chain of eye surgery clinics. A lifelong baseball fan, he was now on a quest to gobble up relics from the golden age of Philadelphia baseball. Between the A's and the Phillies, Shibe Park hosted eight World Series. It also hosted some of the worst teams in league history, but that comes with the territory. Baseball can be a tough business. Unless of course you're the Yankees, but that's a story for another day.

There was a decent crowd around the seats, but I was able to inspect them well enough. These were exactly what the client wanted, but I couldn't act too excited. There were eyes watching me. Circling the seats were the Baker brothers. George and Otis were notorious for working as a team to thwart the bidding goals of other dealers. I found them to be most disagreeable, especially at whatever bar all the dealers ended up in at the end of the day's events. Rumor had it people were headed to the Pink Pony after today's festivities. George spotted me and started in.

"Quick, I didn't expect to see you in Phoenix. You scouting the Shibe seats?"

"Not really. Just looking for chewed gum under these. Got a bout of bad breath."

"Smart ass. You've got a buyer for these things." He looked them up and down. "Looks like a termite hotel, if you ask me."

Otis joined his brother and slapped me on the shoulder. "What's Quickie doing here, George?"

"Claims he's looking for gum. I say he's got his eye on these seats from Philly."

"Morning, Otis. When did you get out?"

"Out of what?"

"Prison?"

He looked around to see who might have heard me say that. "Keep it down. Folks get a little skittish around someone who's been sent up."

"I was just messing with you. You've really done time?"

He pulled me close and whispered. "Remember that auction down in San Antonio?"

"Yeah. What about it?"

"I sort of forgot to give the proceeds to their rightful owners."

"Really, how much did you forget to distribute?"

"All of it."

"Otis! You villain. How long did you get?

"Two years and probation. Served 15 months and then three on house arrest."

I asked, "Was it worth it?"

He grinned and didn't answer. Knowing Otis, he probably lost money once he paid fines and restitution. But in his mind he had stuck it to the man. This of course made me wonder how in the hell he got a badge and number to be in this auction. That stuff tends to follow you. Sure enough, I looked at his badge. "Sylvester Stallone? Seriously, you couldn't come up with a better alias than Sylvester Stallone?"

"You know I love the Rocky and Rambo movies."

"Whatever," I replied. "What are you two bidding on today?"

"Wouldn't you like to know," Otis replied. "Thinking of pushing up that Gehrig jersey."

"Really? Didn't figure you guys for the whale. These seats are more your speed."

"Push off, you douchebag," George replied. "You'll be lucky to scrape enough together to afford these and then blow your profit trying to ship them home. Unless of course, you've already got a buyer?"

"Of course I have a buyer," I said. And so did the Bakers. But we're not going to divulge that because it might give one of us a bidding edge or one of us might try to steal the other's client later. Still, this is the dance and we always seem to do it. "It's the warden of the Texas State Penitentiary," I told the Bakers. "He's expecting a dealer to be making a return visit someday and wants him to feel at home."

"Piss off, Quick." Otis started to walk away.

I called after him. "Come on Otis, that was funny and you know it."

"He's a little sensitive about his time there," George scolded me.

I looked around us before speaking. "Why, because he doesn't want these people to know he went to prison?"

"Not as much as I think he might have been traumatized by his time in there."

"How so?"

"I think he came out a bit confused."

"About what?"

"About himself."

I stared at George for a few moments trying to figure out just what he meant. Then the light bulb went off in my caffeine-deprived mind. "Oh. OH." I watched Otis walk away. "Huh, who would have thought?"

George shrugged and took his leave. "I'll catch up to you later. I need to walk the floor."

The Gehrig crowd had died down and I wedged in for a closer look. I didn't recognize anyone there, and assumed most were single collectors and spectators hoping to catch a glimpse of history. Of course the jersey was under glass, but like I said, I didn't expect any funny business. This was going to be interesting, though. Some of these people were newbies. One wealthy-looking man was talking loud and trying to impress the woman he had hanging on his arm. He was the kind of guy who could muck it up for the rest of us. The combination of being brash and horny was not going to be good for the dealers competing with him. God knows how much he was going to spend in order to get her into bed after the show. She had long fire-red hair and a plunging neckline. Half the other dealers were catching glimpses of her cleavage while the others were listening at him go on about how much money he might spend.

He definitely was a novice, because no expert would dare blurt out that kind of information. A rogue guy like this could make it a bad day for all of us. The rookie dealers were still focused on the girl though. And that was helpful. "I think I might just bid a million for this," the man said.

I rolled my eyes. First, if he was going to bid a million, he was a sucker and an ass. This jersey might get to a million, but no idiot would start there. But a horny fool and his money are soon parted when the command center of thought is below the belt. Typical.

It burned me up. Sure, I'm no saint and I had already had my share of leisurely encounters on this trip. But he was letting sex interfere with business. My business, at that! I couldn't have that happen. I needed to interfere with his business.

"A million, huh?"

He shot me an annoying look. He didn't want anything to distract the bird from his bravado. "Yeah, and more if I have to," he retorted.

"So, you're not bidding on the bed pan?"

"The what?"

"The bed pan. The one Lou Gehrig used in his last days."

"Are you kidding? Who the hell would want to bid on a bed pan?"

"Lots of people. Anybody can get a souvenir from his playing days. But something from his last days, well that's truly unique."

"Is there really a bed pan up for auction today?"

"Of course not. These are respectable people. I looked around and whispered, they don't auction things like that here."

"I'm not interested." He could tell the girl was getting impatient. "I'll stick to the jersey." He brushed against me as he tried to walk past.

"Suit yourself. I'm not bidding on it either. I'm bidding on the crutch."

"The crutch?"

"Mickey Mantle's crutch. The one he used when he was rehabilitating in 1961."

"Who the hell would want a crutch and a bed pan? And where would someone even bid on them," he asked. "eBay?"

He said the word eBay with much disdain. As if it was the Wal-Mart of relic auctions. At this point, I changed tactics. When needed, I can turn on the mystery and charm. Both of which have served me well in the business of sports antiques and in various romantic pursuits. When I answered him, I looked her in the eye. "Do you like to take risks?" She nodded, and he said, "What kind?"

"Would you attend an auction that wasn't entirely legal if the items were so rare and so edgy that nobody could ever walk into your home and say, 'I've got one of those.' " She tilted her head and began to twirl her hair. He tried to move in closer to her so I was addressing him instead of her. I glanced at him, but kept going.

"What if the items were from notorious criminals, murder weapons that had mysteriously been lost by the police after the trial concluded?" I looked her deep in the eyes and said, "Items that were owned by evil men"—I paused for effect—"and notorious women."

She nodded, completely turned on by the idea. Notice I didn't say completely turned on by me. I'm not that arrogant. But some people can become completely turned on by the thought of doing something that is somewhat outside the lines drawn by decent society. She wanted to be a little naughty today. I had recognized it and tapped into that desire. And knowing he wanted to tap into her, I knew all I had to do was sell her on the idea.

He looked at her and gulped. Minutes ago he was bloviating for all to see. Now he was getting squeamish by the thought of attending something that might be illegal. But he was not going to disappoint this woman. His voice was almost shaking. "Just where is this," he gulped, "auction."

Again with a mysterious voice, I replied, "Discretion is, of course, of the utmost concern."

"Of course," she answered for him. She was hooked.

I pulled out a card from my pocket. "Call this number. Give them the code word pterodactyl. They will give you the location and the time."

"Is it today?"

"Later tonight."

"So we can stay for this auction." He was excited, hoping she would give up before he had to drag her to this underground auction.

"I would call that number right away. It could be as far away as Flagstaff or Tucson and you would have to hop in the car and drive there." He winced. I turned back to her, adding "but it will be worth it."

She gave him pleading eyes and asked, "Can we go?"

"Alright, I will give them a call."

As he did, I texted the word "Flagstaff" to Kevin then listened to his end of the call.

"Hello. Yes, it's pterodactyl." A brief pause. "North of Flagstaff? Are you sure? Yes, yes. Thank you."

He turned around to me and the girl who I had been smiling at and admiring while he made the call. "The guy said we need to go to some town north of Flagstaff."

"Too bad," I answered. "I know how much you wanted to see that jersey auctioned off." I then turned my tactic to him in order to seal the deal. "Better off in the long run though."

"How so?"

"Because this is unique," I answered. "You're going to an event that maybe only a handful of people attend. It's the most exclusive auction in America and it only happens three times per year. It's the underground auction for the truly wealthy and discriminating." I turned back to her. "Which you obviously are," I said, smiling at her.

He didn't appreciate my flirting with her, but my words were reeling him in. "Okay, we'll do it." She squealed and gave me a wink.

"Did they give you the address?"

"No, he said they would text it to my number one hour before the auction. But I have to go to Flagstaff right away."

"Then you better go. You don't want to miss this."

They made their way out of the auction area and I pondered just how much money I had saved the rest of the dealers who were bidding today. Bastards, all of them. They owed me a commission for what I might have just saved them. However, it was me who I also saved since I was bidding on it, too. Still, I liked convincing myself that all of these people owed me in some way.

The secret auction ploy had served me well over the years. I don't feel it was particularly evil, more of a Robin Hood sort of crime. The voice on the other end of the line for this guy was my assistant Kevin. He knew if he got a one-word text from me with the name of a city, he was to tell the next person who called to go to that city. Pterodactyl was our way of verifying that the fix was in. Most of the guys we sent on this snipe hunt were high rollers who weren't necessarily in the business. But they represented a certain financial danger to those of us who had a client to make happy. We didn't mind losing to each other nearly as much as we minded losing to these knuckleheads.

"Quick? You bidding on the Gehrig too?" George was back.

"Where did you come from? And no, I'm not bidding on it."

"Oh, then my ears were deceiving me when you sent that sucker and his girlfriend up to Flagstaff?"

I grew slightly embarrassed. "Yeah, well you'll all thank me for that. He was throwing out some crazy numbers for that jersey."

"You also gave yourself away boy. Quickie never sends somebody to the naughty auction unless he's planning to bid on something."

"You're bidding on it too. You and haven't taken your eyes off it since you got here."

"Good luck, Quick."

"You too." I didn't mean it. Not in the least.

At this point, a commotion started in the main vendor area. I moved in the direction of the noise, mostly out of curiosity but also to regroup after George had outed me. I was pissed at myself for letting my intentions slip like that. Still, I had to get rid of the rich guy.

I made my way to the commotion and there was Harry in a robe. Nothing underneath. At first, I tried to hide my face so he couldn't see me. Too late. "Quick, Quick? Where are the rest of the boys?"

Security had been called and they were closing in. "Quick, over here." They confronted him, but didn't want to necessarily grab him, what with the robe being open and his manliness hanging out for the world to see.

A nervous guard said, "Sir, you need to close your robe and come with us."

"What? Kiss my ass," he replied. "Quick, when is it going down?"

At this point, I was afraid they would hear him and take him seriously. I had to move in and make him look senile. What am I saying, he is senile!

"Harry," I said. "What are you doing out of the clinic?"

"Clinic, hell. I'm as right as rain. What are you talking about?"

"Harry, you're in a bathrobe. How did you get here?"

"I took the bus. Same as I do everyday to work."

"Harry you're retired." Okay, I was worried for him too. Thank god his keys had been taken away years ago.

"What time are the strippers getting here?" He licked his lips and rubbed his hands together. "Can't wait to see these girls. Mark my words boy, you aren't going to want to miss this. They're exoticnous?"

"What? That's not even a word."

"The girls. When Hal ordered them, they told him the regular girls were booked but they could send over some that were exoticnous."

"Harry, do you mean androgynous?"

"Yeah, that's it. Androgynous."

I asked, "Do you even know that that means?"

"Yeah, that means they are extra sexy from some foreign place. Probably Portuguese. It sounds Portuguese to me."

"Harry, it's not Portuguese. It means they don't exhibit one particular sex over the other. It means they're gender neutral."

"They're neutered? Like dogs?"

"No, neutral," I replied. "It means they might be dudes."

"No you idiot, we didn't order dudes."

I looked at him for a moment and didn't speak. He went from defiant to disheartened. "Dudes? You're saying we ordered dudes?"

"Not sure, Harry. But yes, you may very well have ordered dudes."

Harry was depressed, sullen and slightly naked. I found Ruben to take care of him and then made my way back to the auction.

The auction started and the first item up was the Shibe seats. So many people were focused on the jersey that I hoped to get this for a near steal. The bidding started at $100. A trickle here and there and we were up to $175. I jumped in at $180. That's when I saw Otis. He was still sore over me outing him for being in prison. His brother may have just outed him for something else. He bid $200 and shot me a snotty grin. Dammit. This was going to cost me. We went back and forth and I wondered where he would stop. I knew he didn't want it, so he would stop somewhere, but I knew he wanted to stick me. Once he got me up to $700, I considered letting it go. He bid $715, and I made like I was going to leave. Now he was sweating, because he didn't have an extra seven bills to drop on this. He had customers and a budget too. They had to be accounted for and he saw today's margin shrinking if he really did have to take this set of seats home. I took a couple of steps and he nearly lost his lunch. started coughing loudly, and I knew that was his signal to come bail him out. I would hold this over him for quite awhile. I bid $720. I waited for a few minutes and nobody responded.

"Sold to Mr. Quick."

I had the seats and since my planned top bid was $1,500, I was going to get a nice commission on this. Now for the Gehrig jersey, after settling up with the auctioneer's staff. I made my way back to the hospitality area and filled out some paperwork. They offered me a fair price to ship it wherever I wanted and I agreed. I did not want to deal with that nonsense!

Chapter Eleven

It took nearly an hour to get to the Gehrig jersey auction. First there were jerseys, bats, signed footballs, helmets, and a variety of relics. The excitement grew with each item. The auctioneer has to keep momentum building. So each artifact is progressively less common and more valuable. In some ways, an auction is like sex. You enjoy the entire experience, but some moments are more pleasurable than others. But regardless of the various activities that lead up to it, everyone is anticipating the big finish.

But now we were at the big finish. And all the dealers were fully aroused, so to speak. I pegged this jersey going for somewhere between $500,000 and $750,000. I felt I had cut $250K off the price just by sending that sucker and his Barbie doll to Flagstaff. I estimated the Baker boys would tap out around $625,000, but I couldn't be certain. I've not known them to work in ranges much higher than that and it was hard for me to believe that somebody hadn't done a background check on Otis . Of course, he was operating as Sly Stallone, but who would believe that?

If I could get it for $650,000, I would make a nice commission of five percent and a bonus of another five thousand. A payday of $37,000 without breaking a sweat. I could beat the Baker boys—I felt confident of that. What I wasn't sure of was who else was lurking about. That is usually where things get sideways.

When I first saw her, I immediately looked for her rich boyfriend or husband. Somebody that amazing undoubtedly would be accompanied by a wealthy collector who was looking to make a splash. I might have to do the Flagstaff con all over again. She wore a white blazer with a crimson blouse underneath. The blazer had faint pinstripes, either dark grey or black—I couldn't say for sure. Her pants matched the jacket and bright red heels matched the blouse.

She stood out from everyone at the auction. I was completely distracted from the proceedings as my eyes kept moving from her to the crowd to see whom she was with. She turned towards me and that's when I noticed she had a wristband and a number. She was bidding! Some new competition had joined us in the form of this spectacular creature. I was excited and terrified at the same time. She wasn't around for the other items, so that meant she was here solely for the Gehrig jersey. Did she (or her client) have the deep pockets it would take to win this auction?

I made eye contact and smiled. She gave a dismissive smile back and looked beyond me to the Baker boys. She eyed them for a moment, then moved her gaze to a couple of well-dressed European looking men standing near the stage. They were pointing and talking very heatedly with each other. It was clear that one wanted to leave and the other wanted to stay and bid.

From there, she sized up a couple of older dealers. They didn't look like much. I had seen these two at a couple of previous auctions. Neither had ever competed for anything this large before. I'm guessing they would throw in a couple of low bids to be able to go back and tell their cronies or clients that they were in the mix for a while. Another younger dealer seemed to have a cameraman following him. Curious, I moved in close enough to hear but not enough to be detected. The young dealer was dressed in a three-piece suit, complete with bow tie and matching pocket square. He was new and looking to make a name for himself. He had the cameraman taking pictures for him to use for his marketing, website, and social media accounts.

I turned back to the woman in white. I was a bit startled because she had approached where I was standing and was just three feet away when I turned around. With heels, she was about an inch taller than me. "Mr. Quick?"

"Yes, that's me. And you are?"

"Valerie. Valerie Westergren."

"Any relation to Raymond Westergren, the auctioneer?"

"I'm his daughter."

"His daughter? Fantastic!" A mutual acquaintance. This might be easier than I thought. "Ray and I used to hang out after the La Jolla shows."

"Mr. Quick, unlike my father, I don't carouse with the competition after the show."

"Ms. Westergen, I've just met you. I'm not the kind of guy to carouse on the first date!"

She began to laugh. "From what I've heard, you're the kind of guy who would carouse in the hospitality tent while the auction is going on."

"Rumors and innuendo. I wouldn't put too much stock in it."

"My father was a drunk and a philanderer. He built an auction empire, then nearly pissed it away drinking and chasing women. I've taken over the family business and I'm not going to make the same mistakes that he made." I really didn't care for the way she looked me up and down when she said mistakes.

"What makes you think I'm like your father?"

"He told me you were!"

"You can't believe him," I replied. "He's a drunk!"

This reply caught her off guard. I had found some sort of judgment loophole for the moment. After a pause she said, "All the same," she said, "I'll not be joining you or any of them at the Pink Pony." She looked around at the other fellas and then stormed off.

I don't think I've ever been that turned on by someone who absolutely despised me. In my mind, I felt I might have rattled her. Clearly she had me rattled when I first saw her. But I had thrown in an argument trump card that had shut her down. Before that, she was on her way to eviscerating me. Which, I suppose, was probably the point.

Within a few minutes, I saw her talking to George Baker. He seemed to get increasingly agitated and eventually threw his hands up in the air and walked off. I wondered what she had used to get to him. She walked away with a smirk on her face.

One by one she picked them off. Short conversations face to face, a whisper in the ear that brought on a shocked reaction. Anything she could do to unnerve the competition. I stood in awe as she worked the room. She didn't even bother with the two older dealers. She knew they were small time. And finally, she made her way to the young new dealer. He was ridiculously easy. I watched her unbutton the top two buttons on her blouse and then let her hair down slowly. Then she put her hand on his shoulder as she asked him a couple of questions. When she was finished, I'll bet he would have bought the jersey for her and carried it to the car.

She was good. And she was dangerous. I was in love, though I should have been in fear. The auction started with a $100,000 minimum bid, which Valerie immediately met. She was sending a message that she was the alpha bidder in a collection of beta males. Fascinating creatures, we humans. The Baker boys jumped it up to $125,000 and she raised it without emotion. The two old guys took turns bidding in $5,000 increments and Valerie topped them. They smiled, nudged each other on the shoulders, then collected themselves to leave. Not only had they bid on a Lou Gehrig jersey, they had been outbid by the most spectacular woman currently breathing in the Phoenix metro area.

Next, the Baker boys moved ahead. The young guy was so enamored with Valerie that he had completely forgotten about bidding. I hoped he wasn't here for a specific client, because there was no way his head was in the game.

Me? I'm a patient bidder. No need to jump in when you have a guess where everyone is going to shake out. I let them waste the energy. And by them I meant the Baker boys. Each bid for them seemed to be an emotional outburst. Valerie, by comparison, remained calm. Too calm, at that. She was an ice queen once the bidding started. She wasn't even flirting with the young guy anymore.

I jumped in when the bid was $250,000. At this point, the increments from the Bakers and the handful of other bidders were consistently in the $5,000 to $10,000 range. I splashed into the pool by shouting $275,000.

Valerie glanced towards me and seemed to see right through me. It was like she was scanning my brain for my top price. "Three hundred fifty thousand" she replied.

"Three hundred seventy five," I answered.

"Four hundred," she came back with.

At this point, the young guy came out of his lust fog and reality set in that the jersey was going to get away. Without any real sense of restraint, he blurted out, "Five hundred thousand."

Valerie shot him a dagger and looked to me to see if I was going to beat him. I was surprised. It was almost as if she had been defeated and she was looking to me to not so much save the day, but at least make sure this guy didn't walk out of there with it.

I topped him at $550,000. He sat back dejected and I figured I had won. Of course, this wasn't the first time I had been taken for a fool by a woman and it won't be the last. That injured kitten look she had given me was just to get me to ferret out the other guy's top dollar. It was obvious he was done and nobody was bidding but the two of us. She was also one step closer to getting my top dollar, which really pissed me off!

She looked me in the eyes again. Gone was the sad eyes and desperation. In their place were the cold eyes of a killer. She looked at me and bid without taking her eyes off of mine: "Five hundred seventy-five thousand."

Two can play this game. I matched her stare and shouted, "Six hundred."

She licked her lips to either try to get under my skin or because she was about to devour me whole. I wasn't sure which. "Six hundred twenty five thousand," she said.

"Six fifty," I shouted back and smiled.

"Seven hundred thousand," she replied.

I must have winced slightly or gave some sort of tell. Because she smiled the most devious of smiles and turned away from me. She was convinced she knew my top dollar and by the smile on her face, she knew she could beat it.

"Seven ten," I shouted. My commission was evaporating and I was getting pissed, but I couldn't let it show. It didn't matter.

She stepped back towards me and whispered, "Mr. Quick. You can nickel and dime me up to 750K, but you and I both know you will top out there. Let me have it for $715,000, and I will throw you a couple of bills for your trouble."

Now can you believe this woman? Trying to buy me out of the game for a measly $200? The nerve. And she knew exactly what my top dollar was. But, I would rather have part of something than all of nothing. "Done."

"Seven hundred fifteen," she called out.

Going. Going. Gone.

I had lost, but maybe had made enough of an impression that I could collect my two bills over dinner and drinks. "Your client obviously had some deep pockets. I didn't know Hector Raven was interested in Yankees relics." Hector was one of her dad's most loyal clients.

"It's not for Hector and even if it was, I wouldn't tell you. Here's your money." She handed me a couple of $100 bills folded together. "Thank you for coming to an understanding."

"How long are you going to be in Phoenix? I would like to catch up and find out what's new with your father's business."

"Catching up implies we have a friendship that needs 'catching up'. We don't. And I'm not staying in Phoenix another second. I'm on a plane in about two hours, so this is where I say goodbye."

"I'll be in San Diego in a couple of months. Maybe we can connect then?"

"Thanks, but as I said, I don't carouse with other dealers."

"Who said anything about carousing? I just wanted to have coffee."

"Coffee, when it involves you, Mr. Quick, almost certainly leads to carousing. Goodbye," she said as she looked out at the floor and back at me, "and good luck."

She walked away, leaving me speechless. I don't know what had me more perplexed. Her comment about good luck or the utter and complete smackdown she had given me. I resolved to look her up in San Diego anyway. I had to figure out what makes her tick before the next time we compete for the same item.

I watched her walking away and just before she reached the doorway of the large hall, a man in a suit approached her. He shook her hand and handed her an envelope. So, this was the buyer. I made my way through the crowd, keeping my eye on him, but making sure she couldn't see me coming. He turned around and pointed towards the stage. Before she could spot me, I ducked into the crowd of a baseball card vendor's booth. Amidst the people and the merchandise, I risked another peek. What I saw horrified me. Valerie's buyer was Carl Byrne.

***

With the auction complete, the event staff quickly went to work setting up the stage for the Byrne Bats announcement. It occurred to me that the Fungo Society would be unveiling its mischief soon. I needed to move to a place that was close enough to see, but far enough away that I couldn't be recognized or attached to whatever was going to happen in any way. I moved to a good viewing angle from the food court. I would be able to see and hear it all from the public address/video system.

The crew rolled in a structure to hold lights and the smaller stage that was used for the auction was quickly switched out for a taller and more imposing one. Byrne Bats staffers swarmed the place. Some were hanging banners and other point of sale items. A team of women in green polos and short shorts was passing out swag to anyone walking by. No sign of Byrne himself yet, but media folks were setting up cameras and microphones. A giant green podium was set up with the Byrne Bats company logo on the front.

Nine chairs were set up on the stage. When everything was ready, more women in the same outfits led eight ballplayers out onto the stage. Each wore the jersey of his respective team as well as a green Byrne baseball hat. The crowd that had assembled cheered loudly. As more people poured in, I had to stand up to see the stage clearly.

I noticed Rainbow first. He gave me a sly wink, but didn't say anything to me. I caught a glimpse of Tommy in the crowd near the stage. He was wearing sunglasses, which of course drew attention to him.

After the players were seated, Byrne came out with a girl on each side who accompanied him to his seat in the middle. After the girls left the stage, the convention organizer came out and went directly to the podium. He thanked the crowd, introduced all the players, and finally introduced Byrne.

It's hard to describe in words, but even his walk was arrogant. But he could command the crowd. "Ladies and gentlemen, we are proud to be here and proud of the advances that Byrne has made over the years. As you know, we don't have the only bats in Major League Baseball, but we do have the best. In our never-ending pursuit of the most technically advanced tools for our athletes, we have once again reengineered the modern wood bat."

I can't believe how full of BS this guy is. "Today we announce that our Dublin Doubleday bats have been approved for use in MLB play." The crowd applauded. "We are debuting the bats this season and the first action you will see them in will be when the men behind me take the plate on March 17, Saint Patrick's Day!"

More applause. "Each one of these leadoff batters will be swinging a special green-painted St. Patrick's Day edition of the Dublin Doubleday. Ladies, let's unveil the bat!"

Two of the ladies rolled out a small cart that was covered in a green cloth with the Byrne Bats logo on it. They pulled it away and revealed a solitary green bat. Byrne held it up and everyone did their customary oohs and aahs. I was pretty far away, but judging by the excitement from the crowd up front and the players, it was an impressive piece of lumber.

It was at this point that the event took a rather bizarre turn. When the big reveal occurred, the PA was playing grandiose, stadium style rock and roll to get the crowd moving. Suddenly, the music stopped for a moment, then restarted with Boy George singing "Do You Really Want to Hurt Me?"

Everyone looked around to see if this strange interruption would be quickly fixed. It wasn't. Instead, four very androgynous-looking men in hot pants took the stage and began to dance. Byrne had to fight off the initial shock in order to muster a "What the hell?"

The baseball players who were Cuban, having no real command of English and not entirely sure why they were here, started dancing with the men. They just assumed this was part of whatever this American businessman was paying them to do and they were happy to play along, knowing a paycheck would be forthcoming.

At this point, it became harder for the emcee and Byrne to put a stop to it because the American players figured they had missed a memo and didn't want to be the only ones not dancing. It was ugly and awkward, but the players tried their best to keep up with the professionals. This was all too much for the crowd to comprehend. Most of the media were trying to make sense of how the new bats, St. Patrick's Day, and male dancers shared a common thread, but were too afraid to ask the Byrne media team for fear of being labeled intolerant. The media team members too afraid to say anything and praying to God nobody would ask until somebody from the C-Suite told them what the hell was going on. In this holding pattern, nobody moved and nobody tried to stop the dancing.

Upping the ante, the dancers began to take their clothes off and smoke bombs began pouring clouds of blue and green onto the stage. At first, the bizarre nature of everything that led up to this caused the audience not to react. They thought the smoke was part of the show. After a minute or so, people started to realize that someone or several some ones were lighting the smoke bombs and setting them off in the crowd. People began to rush for the exits. Several old men were huddled in the corner opposite me, laughing.

Byrne was understandably angry and looking for who was responsible. He began yelling at one of the staff, who pointed to the corner with the old guys. They were no longer there. Out in the vendor section, however,

Tommy was being detained by the police. I saw the cuffs go on him before the smoke was more than I could stand. I made my way out of the convention center and quickly walked to my rental car. They guys had successfully disrupted the event, but I wondered what they had really managed to accomplish.

The next morning, I found out they hadn't managed to accomplish much. The TV news highlights all seemed to cut off at the bat reveal. Byrne had used his clout to suppress any mention of the strange shenanigans after the reveal. As for the Internet, that was another story. The LGBT community was already adopting the Dublin Doubleday as the most tolerant bats in baseball. The Fungos were depressed. Their mission had failed.

***

I called Rainbow to see if Tommy was still in jail and if he had given up any of the other guys. Rainbow said Tommy had pulled the senile routine and had convinced the cops that he hadn't lit the smoke bomb, but had inadvertently picked it up. They must get a lot of disoriented seniors in Phoenix because the cops bought his story and let him go.

However, the Fungos were not satisfied with their prank, as it seemed not to have made any impact on the public's perception of Byrne Bats. Instead, it might very well have opened a new market to the company.

They were determined to find a new way to strike back at Byrne. I was determined to find out more about Valerie Westergren. In the meantime, I made arrangements to get the Musial jersey to its new owner. Rainbow was supposed to meet me for breakfast back at the hotel, so I returned after shipping the jersey. Ramona met me at the hotel door.

"Mr. Baseball. I didn't see you at all yesterday. And the night staff said a taxi dropped you off at 1 a.m. Where were you?"

Really? I couldn't believe I was getting the third degree. "I told you I had to work at the convention all day."

"And what about last night? They said you were drunk."

"Why do you have hotel employees spying on me?"

"They are not spying. But they are watching."

"Well, tell them to stop watching. Didn't they tell you I came home alone?" Surprisingly, after a night with the other dealers, I hadn't woken up with a hangover. Now, I had one.

"Yes, they did. But you were out till one. Nothing good happens at one in the morning." The angrier she gets, the more her English reverts to Spanish.

"Look, I like you but you have to stop being paranoid. I have to hang out with other dealers. It's how we trade information. It's how we learn about potential clients, uncover info about relics."

"With alcohol after midnight? I don't believe it."

"Yes, with alcohol. Sometimes that's when people let their guard down."

She looked straight at my crotch. "Don't you be letting your guard down, Mr. Baseball. You might find your guard is missing when you wake up." She looked down there again. Crazy. Can you believe it? Why do I always manage to sniff out the craziest woman in any town I visit in America?

Chapter Twelve

The next day I met a half dozen or so Fungos at Peoria Sports Park for a Royals/Padres game. We filed into seats behind the Padres dugout and watched the teams warm up. Within a few minutes, a group of guys sat across the aisle from us and began talking with the players. It was the same group we had seen before at Camelback Ranch.

I decided to learn more about the bat businesses and introduced myself to the guy who seemed to be in charge. "Are you guys from one of the bat companies?"

"Yes, Mine Bats. I'm Pete O'Brien, the owner."

"Nice to meet you I'm Quick."

"Quinn?"

"No, Quick. Jonathan Quick. You can call me Quick. Tell me about your bats."

He went on to tell me about how they were at their first spring training. The company had been around for about seven years, but it took five years of going through MLB's hoops in order to have Mine Bats on the field.

During that time, the company had to submit bats for testing and make modifications based on MLB's specs. There was something exciting about watching this small business trying to hustle a living at spring training.

Apparently the Mine reps had scored access to the Padres practice the day before and several of the players had agreed to try the bats out today. Still, some were a little reticent so each batter who had a Mine Bat was receiving a pep talk from the bat guys.

Pete told me about Mine's bats and how the company used beechwood instead of ash or maple. He told me to listen for the sound of the ball coming off the bat and how it differed from other bats. I think I heard it. I'm not really sure. But I liked the look of the bats and enjoyed learning all about the process.

I asked him about the Byrne Company. "So, what do you know about the Byrne bats?"

"They're huge. Not Louisville Slugger huge, but they have about 20 percent of the market and they are looking to make a huge move this year."

"How so?"

"They have a new model, not sure what type of wood. But they are debuting it on St. Patrick's Day." He pulled out a flyer and handed it to me. It was from Byrne Bats. "They got permission to let their endorsees use green bats on St. Patty's Day. The new bats won't be green for regular game play, but they will debut in green. The unique thing is that they have secured—at great expense—deals with the likely leadoff hitter for each visiting team that day. Their plan is to livestream the first at-bat at every game using the new bat model."

"Wow, that's a pretty big splash."

"Yeah, we don't have the deep pockets to pull that off," Pete said. "We're just going to be happy if we can get a handful of players to agree to use our bats in the regular season. It's very competitive though."

"So how much do you think Byrne has sunk into this promotion?"

"Rumor has it, he has mortgaged the farm to make this happen. He's spent all kinds of money to promote the livestream, more to sign all the hitters, even more to bribe the managers to make sure those guys are in the lineup and batting first. I wouldn't be surprised if he even paid the pitchers to throw them fastballs down the middle. Of course, that would be like the Black Sox scandal all over again, but that's the type of guy he is."

"How much money could this mean for his company?"

"Bumping his share of the market from 20 percent to 40 percent would mean about $10 million in revenue. That's not chump change."

"And if it fails?"

"Well, see, now you're on to something because I was thinking about that myself."

"How so?"

"Think about if it failed somehow. What if it rained?"

"In Phoenix?"

"Okay, but think if there was some unusual reason that games were postponed," Pete continued. "Come the next day, those same teams aren't in the same ballparks or playing the same teams. In other words, different guys could be hitting leadoff and he simply doesn't have the cash left to buy off more of them."

"Really?"

"Yes, and I hear he's leveraged to the hilt with his other businesses."

"The real estate?"

"Exactly! All his eggs are in this basket. If this fails, his whole empire could topple."

"Interesting. What about the bats themselves? What would happen if the bats were faulty in some way?"

"Not likely, given all the testing we have to go through. But from my understanding, the bats are going to be shipped to Phoenix on the 15thor 16th MLB will run a quick test on them, and then they will be delivered to the ballparks for the 17th."

"What kind of tests will they run?"

"Not the kind of rigorous tests that we usually have to go through. The bats are already approved, but since these are a special batch, painted in green, they will check them for weight, length, etc."

"Will anyone hit with them during the test?"

"No, they'll just do the weights and measures."

"Do you know where this testing is being done?"

"Yes, because we were asked to do special light blue and pink ones for Mark Leonard of the Rangers. His wife just had twins, a boy and a girl."

"So, you know where the facility is. Have you already taken your bats there?"

"No, I'm going tomorrow."

"Would you be willing to let me go with you? It would help me with research on bats."

"Research?"

"Yeah, anything I can do to learn how bats are made and how they are altered can help me spot fakes in my line of work."

"Just what is your line of work?"

"I find artifacts."

"Bats are artifacts?"

"They are when they are 100 years old and used by players from the deadball era."

"Ever search for newer items?"

"When the money is right."

"So what are you looking for right now?"

I thought it better not to tell him about the Ruth jersey. The fewer people who knew about that the better.

"I'm looking for a 1969 Royals jersey."

"Worth a lot of money?"

"No, not a great paying gig either. But, it's more about doing someone a favor."

"A woman?"

"Well sort of. And her dad."

"Her dad?"

"Yeah, I found his pants."

He looked at me sort of strange. "Don't go too far. I need to talk to the guy on deck, and then I want to continue this."

***

After the game, Rainbow and I followed the bat guys out to the stadium parking lot. We made our way to a minivan. I thought we were going to a giant truck covered in logos. Instead, this was a rented minivan crammed with bats and empty fast food bags. These guys were truly bootstrapping. I wondered if they were even sleeping in the van.

"Take a cut with one of these," Pete said, handing Rainbow a bat. He caressed the wood.

"I've never seen anything like it," Rainbow said. "It doesn't have a sheen to the finish. It's a matte finish."

"What do you think?"

I took the bat, stepped back away from the group and took a few swings. Without batting gloves, you got a real sense of the feel of the wood. Like Rainbow, I thought it felt different than any bat I had ever held or swung. "I love the feel. It's a unique grip," I told them.

The bat guys spent another twenty minutes selling us on the virtues of the bat, from durability to spring. I was convinced. I wanted to swing one in a batting cage. They agreed to take me with them to the Brewers camp later in the week. Ruben tried to keep the bat, but they had a limited number of samples. We thanked them for their hospitality and said our goodbyes.

Leaving the stadium, Rainbow asked me, "You seemed to have a lot of questions for that guy. You're up to something, aren't you?"

"What makes you say that?"

"All that stuff about when the bats arrive, will they hit with them? You're thinking of sabotaging those bats, aren't you?"

"Now that you mention it, the thought crossed my mind," I admitted, smiling.

"I knew it! If we could make all those bats break on the first at-bat, every freaking one of them, we would ruin that son-of-a -bitch!"

"Don't get ahead of yourself. Yes the thought crossed my mind, but I don't have any idea how we could get the bats, alter them somehow, and do it in such a way that the sabotage could not be detected."

"Do you know anyone at Byrne Bats?"

"No, do you?"

"No, but it seems to me that we will have to get the exact green paint they used in order to cover up our tracks," Ruben said.

"You're right. There has to be somebody in the Fungo Society who has a connection there. We also need to make sure that they can't track this back to us. We're going to need a disgruntled Byrne employee."

Ruben laughed, "From everything we know about the guy, that shouldn't be hard."

"Okay, if we can get the paint, and get the bats, do we sabotage them before MLB looks at them, or after?"

"Why take a chance? Let's bypass the process altogether."

"What do you mean?"

"How about we intercept them before they get to the ballparks and then deliver them ourselves?"

"Won't MLB be expecting them?"

"Sure, but we give them a different set of bats."

"That won't work. He can claim that the bats that break in the game weren't his. No, for this to work, these need to be Byrne Bats."

"Well, it was just a thought."

"No, I think you're on to something," I told Ruben. "We just need to figure out how to intercept the bats, alter them, paint them, and then deliver the bats while making MLB think they looked at the bats."

"You think we can do it?"

"How much money does the Fungo Society have?"

"How much are we going to need?"

"We need a wood guy. The best I know. We're going to have to fly him to Phoenix right away. And we're going to need a shop with all the tools he needs to fix these bats."

"We'll make it work."

"Okay, when we get back to the hotel, I will call George and get him packing for Arizona. You get with all the Fungo guys and see if anyone has a contact—disgruntled or otherwise—who works at Byrne's bat factory. We need that paint!"

"What about MLB and the measurements?"

"I haven't figured that out yet."

"By the way," Ruben asked me. "What changed your mind?"

"What do you mean?"

"You've been hesitant to support our revenge on Byrne. What changed?"

"I lost an auction to him."

"You lose auctions all the time."

"Yeah, but he didn't fight fair."

"Was he part of a bidding ring?" A bidding ring happens when a group of bidders conspire together to keep the price low. They bid only against outsiders and once the hammer falls, they hold an unofficial auction amongst themselves. Then the difference in price is split between the members of the ring. And you thought there wasn't any intrigue in the collectible world.

"No, something much more treacherous: a woman."

"A woman?"

"Yes, she worked the room, picked us all off one by one and then shook hands with Byrne just moments after the hammer fell."

"Are you sure? If Byrne is leveraged to the max, where is he getting money for a high priced relic like that jersey?"

"I don't know, but now it's personal."

***

Rainbow dropped me off at the hotel. I glanced at the front desk and was relieved that Ramona was nowhere to be found. I went up to my room to contact George. George is a master craftsman. If it's made of wood, George can do it. I use him for jersey frames and other display cases. The types of artifacts I hunt shouldn't rest in a case from the local hobby store. These items need cases with artistry and craftsmanship. And George was the best.

I called him right away. "George, this is Quick."

"How can I help you?"

"I need you to modify some bats."

"How many?"

"About thirty."

"No problem, just bring them by the shop."

"Can't do that. I need you to come to the bats."

"And just where are the bats?"

"Scottsdale, Arizona."

"Are you drunk?"

"No, I'm completely serious. Before we settle that, though, did Eddie Sloane ever have you work on the frame you built for him? I noticed it had been modified."

"He called me once and asked some questions about the specs. Said he had cracked the glass and damaged the fabric and wanted to replace it. But he didn't send it to me. He just had a local guy do it."

Another dead end. "Okay, well I need you in Phoenix and these guys will pay well."

It took a little convincing, but George agreed to come to Phoenix for a sizable fee. He also had a cousin who built cabinets in Foxdale. So, we had our wood guy and we had our workshop.

Rainbow called a little later and was pleased to announce that Dave knew someone at Byrne Bats. That someone was a salesman for the southwest territory. He had been informed that he was too old for the road and was being phased out at the end of March. He was the perfect mole. Disgruntled, chip on his shoulder, and willing to be discreet. He had told Dave he was certain that he could get a sample of the paint and bring it with him. He was flying from Texas to Phoenix the next morning.

Now we had the wood guy, we had the shop and we had the paint. So, it was on me to figure out how to intercept the bats and deliver something to MLB that they could certify. I spent about thirty minutes thinking about possible ideas when I got a call form Ramona. She wanted me to meet her at a bar. I wanted her to come up to my room. She said she couldn't be seen coming to a guest's room. I decided that an evening with Ramona might clear my head. Of course, it also could muddy the waters even more. So, I tried to have a serious adult conversation with her about what this relationship was all about. Seriously, I really gave it the old college try. However, my Spanish isn't nearly as good as my French.

Chapter Thirteen

"Quick has an idea." Rainbow had convened the Fungo Society at Denny's again and was starting to tell them my plan. I really don't know how these old guys have so much energy in the morning. I was dragging. The only thing propping me up was coffee and coffee with a side of coffee.

"For what?" asked Hank.

Rainbow answered, "For how we can pay back that son-of-a-bitch."

"How?"

"Well, he's making this big deal about how on March 17th, every leadoff hitter at all the spring training games will hit with a Byrne bat," I said.

"Yeah, so?" answered Tommy.

"So we sabotage those bats to break," I continued. "Imagine if all eight batters broke their bats. It would be the worst publicity ever."

"I'm sure some fans and players would notice, but it's just a spring training game. How much damage could that do," asked Scooter.

Rainbow answered. "Because the pompous ass is going to show it on the interweb, that's why? People all over the country are going to be watching."

"The interweb," asked Hank.

"He means the Google," Scooter answered.

Hal asked, "The Google? Isn't that what Lefty White called his curve ball?"

"No, the Google was that bird in Chicago's front office who had the thick eyeglasses. Blind as a bat, but she sure liked to party," said Tommy.

"Her nickname wasn't the Google. She was called the…" Scooter said.

Rainbow shouted, "YouTube! That's what they are going to watch it on."

"YouTube? What the hell is that?" asked Hal.

"It's the Internet, Hal," I interjected. "Don't you ever go online to see what your grandkids are doing?"

"No, the missus read there was porn on the Internet," said Hal. "Won't let it in the house"

"Let's get back to St. Patty's Day," I said. "Byrne is going to have all the first at-bats simultaneously broadcast on his website."

"How do we get all those guys' bats and sabotage them," asked Scooter. "We would have to do multiple bats per guy because each has three to four of them. Plus they would notice if we started messing with them."

"We don't have to get their bats. MLB approved a green St. Patrick's Day bat for that day. Each leadoff hitter for the visiting team will get one delivered—and one only—the day of the game. They've been instructed to not use it in BP so it has no nicks when they come up to bat. It's in their contracts with the bat company. So, all we have to do is intercept the bats, alter them and get them to all the ballparks."

"Oh, and I thought you said it would be hard. You putz, how the hell are we supposed to intercept all those bats," Rainbow said.

"I'm working on it," I said. "Give me some time."

"What if someone 'official' had to weigh and measure those bats before they were used? We could make the switch then."

"No, we can't switch them out for bats that aren't theirs," I insisted. "They have to be altered versions of their bats."

"Will this really make a difference? They will know that someone sabotaged them. How is this really going to hurt their business?"

"It's all about perception," I explained. "Once other players see those bats breaking on the first at-bat, they aren't going to want to give them a try. Even if they know the bats were tampered with, the visual is still there in their minds. The damage will be done. No player wants to be associated with a laughingstock."

"I agree," said Scooter, "and for that reason, the bats shouldn't just break."

"What do you mean," I asked.

Scooter continued. "They should fail, but in a dramatic way. What if when they cracked, confetti exploded out of the bat?"

"That would be dramatic," said Tommy.

"Damn straight!" Hal couldn't keep himself from yelling.

"Can you imagine," Rainbow said, warming to this twist. "All those eyes on the bats? Green and white confetti spraying all over home plate and the umpire? Byrne will shit himself." Rainbow rubbed his hands together and grinned, a noticeable habit whenever he is really excited.

"Nobody would ever pick up one of their bats again," said Scooter. "He would be ruined."

"But is it even possible?" asked Hank.

"I think I know a way," I answered. "But we have to get those bats in our hands. We'll need about three days."

At this point, a few of the Fungos started to have second thoughts. "I don't know guys, I've already been to jail once over this," said Frank.

"Gentlemen, it comes down to this. Are we going to get revenge for Eddie or not," asked Rainbow.

"What is revenge going to do for us?" asked Tommy.

"More importantly, what is it going to do for Eddie?" asked Frank. "It's not going to do anything for anyone. It's just going to make us feel better for an hour or so, and then everything will be the same. His wife will still be in the nursing home. His daughter will still not have a whole lot of cash to take care of her with, and Eddie will still be dead."

Rainbow fired right back. "Really? Did you really have to bring us all down like that? These guys are tough enough to motivate as it is without you coming in and being a wet blanket."

"I'm just trying to be realistic. Besides, I didn't say I didn't want to do it. I just don't think it's going to change anything."

"When that prick Nolan Ryan hit Tommy in '73 and we cleared the benches did it solve anything?"

"No, but I think Frank broke his finger," said Tommy.

"Not my point. Did we solve anything?"

"No."

"Did it change the fact that Tommy couldn't finish the game?"

"No!"

Rainbow continued, "But would any of you, if you had to go back in time to that very day, not get off that bench and not throw a few punches?"

A chorus of noes erupted from the Fungos.

"And you want to know why?" He paused. "Because it felt damn good to go out there and defend one of our own. We did it because Tommy was one of us. We did it for honor. For duty."

"What's your point," asked Hal.

"My point is, dammit, we're doing this. We are not letting Eddie down!"

"Look, I'm all for honor and all that stuff, but we could go to jail for this. The worst thing that could happen to us for a bench-clearing brawl is we get suspended for a couple of games. I don't want to go to jail," said Frank.

"You're not going to go to jail!" Ruben didn't want his pep talk deflated.

Scooter laughed, "Hank wouldn't mind going to jail and getting away from that old hen he lives with."

"Old hen, that's no way to talk about Hank's wife," said Tommy.

Scooter piled on, "You're only defending her because you used to live with her, too."

I looked at Hank and looked at Tommy. "Huh?"

"What did you say?" asked Hank.

Scooter looked at Tommy. "Oh, Hank didn't know about you two?"

"What the hell are you trying to say," Hank demanded.

"Tommy and Bea lived together in '65, before you were traded to Kansas City."

"Ah, you guys are putting me on. She never told me about ..." Hank looked at Tommy, who ducked his head. "You son of a bitch! You were sleeping with my wife!" Hank took a swing at Tommy with his cane.

"Well she wasn't your wife then." Tommy tripped over Hal's walker trying to get away. Hank jumped on him, then screamed, "My back!"

Two old men, alternating between yelling at each other and yelling in pain. It was hard to watch. Any confidence that this enterprise would be successful went out the window. I lifted my plate just before they fell onto the table in front of me. I took a bite of my eggs, then grabbed my coffee before they spilled it.

I took a sip and then spoke loudly over the screams of the two men on my table. "Rainbow, maybe this isn't the group you want to use to pull this off."

They stopped fighting each other for a moment. "What are you saying," asked Hank.

"Yeah, what the hell does that mean," added Tommy.

I must have struck a nerve. With each other, there was sparring and constant antagonizing. But any threat from the outside, any perceived diss, was met with a unified defiance. I had just unified them.

Tommy asked, "You thinking of backing out on us, Jersey Man?"

"Jersey Man?"

"Yeah, Jersey Man. You afraid of a little danger? Possibility of jail time going to make you run home to mommy," said Hank.

"Now come on guys. You've got to admit that none of you are master criminals. Just how do you think you're going to pull this off? Hal's on an oxygen machine, for heaven's sake! No offense, Hal."

Rainbow took over. "That's exactly why they won't see it coming. And why the police won't look our way when it's over. We're old. Washed up. Put out to pasture. Nobody thinks we matter anymore. And guys like Byrne can take down guys like Eddie because he's certain that his teammates are too old to get off the bench and start swinging."

Heads were nodding. A few eyes teared up. Not mine of course, but somebody's eyes. "Well, I'm not staying on the bench. I'm getting up. And even if it takes me a half hour to go from the dugout to the mound, I'm going to march out there and knock that smug smile off of Ryan's face, " Hal said.

"Byrne's face," I added.

"Him too."

"I'm in."

"Me too."

"Let's bury the bastard."

A chorus of "I'm in" and "let's do it" chimed in from the rest of the Fungos.

"Okay," said Hal. "Let's go take a nap."

The guys got up and filed out the door. "Hey, where are they going? We didn't plan the heist," I said.

Scooter answered, "Oh, Rainbow was on a roll. He got them so fired up, I guess they forgot. Best to let them go. They're used to a schedule."

Rainbow and I met up later in the day in my hotel lobby. After breakfast, Scooter had put me in touch with an old scout who worked for Byrne. Scooter told me the scout wasn't happy and wouldn't need much convincing to be our inside guy. "Our mole inside Byrne Bats is going to escort the bats to Phoenix. He's going to switch the bag with us at the airport after Byrne himself meets him at the airport to confirm they have arrived."

"What if he takes them into his possession there?"

"He won't. He's relying on the mole to get them to each stadium. Once he's seen them in person, the mole is supposed to take them to his hotel and lock them up. Then he is supposed to be on the road at 7 a.m. to deliver to all eight ballparks. So, we have from 4 p.m. the day before until 7 a.m. to fix the bats. That includes a half hour each way to George's workshop where we will work on them."

"That's basically 14 hours to doctor how many bats?"

"Thirty. There are thirty guys using the green bats on St. Patty's Day. Not all of them are leading off, true. But we need to make sure the bats look the same. If we refinish the doctored ones, they might look different than the ones we don't touch. If we doctor all of them, they won't be able to tell if they were sabotaged at the factory."

"Can he do 30 bats in one night?"

"It's going to be close. We're going to have to do an assembly line. And we're going to have to work all night," I said. "Now, I want some of the guys to be at the ballparks on the day of the event. Some of them will be on the assembly line. Do any of them have a son or grandson who can help?"

"I don't think we want to expose anybody else to the legal risk of this," Rainbow said.

"We just need a team to work through the night. You think these guys can do it?"

Rainbow paused. "I see your point. Does George have an assistant?"

"Yes, his nephew, but it will cost more."

"Do we have to do all of those bats in one night? Any chance the mole can come a day early?"

"No, he can't. If he was a day earlier, Byrne could deliver some of them himself. This way, he can't and has to rely on the mole."

"Okay, we will have to rely on George's nephew, too."

We both sat quietly for a few minutes. Eventually my mind went back to the Ruth jersey.

"What are you thinking" Rainbow asked.

"What if Eddie never sold the Ruth jersey? What if he put it in the original frame I had George make for the Royals jersey and tried to pass it off as a cheap replica?"

"Why on earth would he do that?"

"So he could temporarily loan it to someone, planning on getting it back someday. Remember the jersey in his wife's room at the nursing home? His daughter said that when her mother passes, all of the memorabilia he loaned to the nursing home comes back to her. Maybe the Ruth jersey is hanging somewhere in that nursing home and nobody has a clue what it actually is?"

"That's pretty thin."

"Wait, there's more. I've been thinking about the land price discrepancy and the jersey receipt. What if Eddie pretended to sell the jersey and underreported the money he got for the land so they balanced out."

"I'm not following you."

"If he sold the land for $1,000,000 but claimed to sell the jersey for $500,000 and the land for $500,000, most people aren't going to catch it because there is still a million dollars in his bank account, right?"

"Yeah, I suppose."

"Then Eddie keeps the jersey, has someone at KC Collectibles make him a fake receipt or makes it himself, and nobody knows the truth. Then he hides it in his donated collection so that his daughter gets it when he dies."

"That still doesn't explain why he was upset over losing the Royals jersey," Rainbow said.

"Dammit, I was on a roll! Don't do that when I'm on a roll!"

Rainbow looked hurt.

"You're right," I said. "We're back to square one."

After a few seconds of silence, Rainbow spoke. "We can at least go back to the nursing home and look for the jersey."

"Yeah, that sounds like a good idea. Things are getting a little dicey around here." I glanced at the front desk. "Maybe we should check out the nursing home and then hit a game."

"Woman troubles?" he looked at Ramona, then back at me. I nodded. "You're a walking tabloid paper, Quick. When are you going to settle down and get married?"

"And miss all this kind of fun? Rainbow, you surprise me."

We made our way towards the main door of the hotel. Ramona was watching us, just daring me with her eyes to walk by without speaking. "I'll catch you outside in a moment, take my keys and get the air conditioning going." I tossed Rainbow the keys and approached Ramona.

"Good morning."

"It's about time you speak to me. How long were you going to ignore me today?"

Doesn't that beat everything? I give her some space and time to handle the customers and all she can do is complain.

"I was trying to be polite and not interrupt you while you were working. Of course I'm not avoiding you."

"We need to talk. Wait here, and I will get someone to cover the desk."

"I can't stay right now. We have to go to the nursing home."

"Liar! You're going to see that slut!"

"Slut? What slut?"

"Jessica Slut. The one who leaves you messages. The one who came into my lobby looking like a slut."

"Messages. As in there was more than one?"

"Yes, but I threw them away."

"Why? I'm not trying to sleep with her! This is my job!"

"Your job is to associate with sluts? I don't like her. You need a new job."

"Ramona, I've got to go."

"Fine, go to your slut."

I turned around and who was standing behind me? Mrs. Middle America. Hands on her daughter's ears again. I tried to apologize, really I did. But I didn't do it so well.

"I'm not really going..."

"Pervert!"

"This is really just a misunderstanding. I'm sorry you and your daughter had to hear this."

"This is a family hotel! I think you should leave."

"But I..."

"Good day sir!"

At first I was feeling guilty about what the woman had to hear, but her attitude pissed me off. So I left her with this, "I'll just go to my slut now." Of course, Ramona heard this and started cursing at me in Spanish.

Rainbow and I got to the nursing home and split up. I made up a story for the nursing home director about the donated memorabilia being featured in a story by the Hall of Fame for its monthly magazine and she bought it pretty easily. There were four wings to the facility, so the process took a while.

We probably could have made it in about an hour. But this being a nursing home, every room we entered, every hallway ventured into brought a new senior wanting to chat. It's a sad place. So many people in the twilight of their lives, just desperate for someone to listen.

I was quite pleased to hear that one gentleman considered these the good old days. He recently had discovered Viagra and had become an absolute hound in the Bob Hope Hallway of Wing 3 in the Cozy Cactus Senior Home. His name was Ted Leonard and he had worked in a silver mine when he was twenty. It took me 45 minutes to get out of Ted's room as he alternated stories about silver mining and mining for silver foxes in the Cozy Cactus.

Room after room, I was welcomed to sit and visit. It was too hard to just peek in, look for the jersey and leave. One woman told me she was a secretary to President Truman. I have no way of knowing if this was true, as she was in the dementia ward, but it made for a good story.

Finally, I caught up with Rainbow. He'd had no luck either. The Babe Ruth jersey was nowhere to be found in the Cozy Cactus. At this point, I had to let the Babe Ruth theory go and focus on the Royals jersey. Maybe the change in the background fabric was nothing. Maybe Eddie spilt something on it and had to change it. Dwelling on it wouldn't get me any closer to the Royals jersey and that's the one that had a definable return on investment. The Ruth jersey was a unicorn.

The nursing home took so long we missed most of the game we had planned to see that day. But we still went to the ballpark and caught the last two innings. Baseball was happening. We had to be a part of it.

Chapter Fourteen

Who is Moonlight Graham? Well, Archibald "Moonlight" Graham is the most famous player to ever play an inning and a half of baseball. People will tell you it was only one inning, but technically it was one and a half. Not that that matters. What's important is that a man by the name of W.P. Kinsella was doing research for a book and noticed an entry in The Baseball Encyclopedia about this guy who played an inning and didn't get to hit.

He found the concept fascinating, so he went all the way to Chisholm, Minnesota, to learn about this former baseball player. Turns out, Moonlight Graham was known as Doc Graham to the folks in Chisholm and he was revered as a kind and generous benefactor. Kinsella loved the story and weaved Graham's life into his best selling book Shoeless Joe. That book became the basis for the movie Field of Dreams starring Kevin Costner.

Ever since the movie came out and exposed the Moonlight Graham story to a wide audience, people have been fascinated by his life. So, you would think finding an artifact from his playing days would be easy, right? Not so fast. Graham played in the early 1900s. Player jerseys didn't have numbers until 1920. Shoeless Joe, the novel, didn't come out until 1982, and the film adaptation was released in 1989. Meaning nobody heard of Archie Graham until the '80s, and that meant nobody would have been actively seeking or collecting anything that might have belonged to him for more than 70 years since he retired from the game.

The odds that somebody had a jersey from a no-name player on a forgotten minor league team from pre-1910 were worse than winning the lottery. Besides, you're probably thinking that collectors and dealers had turned over every stone to find a jersey or some relic. And you would be right. But I hadn't put my mind to it. And I was pretty confident in my ability to turn over the right stone.

That doesn't mean I didn't have my work cut out for me. I had four options: the Scranton Minors, the Charlotte Hornets, the Binghamton Bingoes, and the Memphis Egyptians—all teams that Graham played for.

Thank God for the Internet. If I had to search for a Moonlight Graham artifact without it, it might have taken a decade. Now of course, you wouldn't just find the jersey on eBay, although I did start there. I managed to find a great picture of Graham and his Scranton teammates. Of course it was in black and white, but I could at least get an idea of jersey style and lettering.

Next I went with a few Google searches to see if I could find any of the other jerseys.

Finally, I called the master. There is one man in America who has done the most comprehensive research on minor league jerseys of the past. From professionals to semi-pro, American to Latin America to Japan, one man is the encyclopedia of jerseys: Jerry Klapper. Jerry owns a store in Seattle, Washington, called Vintage Flannels. The store sells authentic reproductions of just about any minor league jersey in history. They make them with the same materials (wool flannel, felt lettering, authentic sleeve patches, etc.) and designs that were used in times past.

If anyone had a picture of a jersey from any of these teams it would be Jerry. If anybody would have an idea on how I could track down a jersey, it would be him.

"Jerry, it's Quick."

"Please don't tell me you want me to fake a jersey. I've told you that's not what we do!"

"Jerry, come on. I wouldn't think of it. It was only that one time and it was life or death!"

"You destroyed a framed Joe DiMaggio jersey. A San Francisco Seals one at that!"

"Hey, I didn't know the team owner's daughter was going to force herself on me right there in the conference room."

"You told me it was an assistant!"

"She was. And she happened to be the owner's daughter. But it's not my fault she ripped off my shirt and shoved me against the wall."

"Are you sure it wasn't the other way around?

"Hand to God, Jerry. Hand to God."

"So what do you want today?"

"I'm looking for a jersey. Circa 1904-1907. Scranton, Charlotte, Binghamton or Memphis. Minor league, no fakes, I promise. I need to know if you've ever had a special order for one of these and if so, do you have a photo? Also, if you were able to produce these, you must have had some source material. I need that material or access to it. I need to track down an authentic jersey from one of those teams in one of those years."

"That's going to be hard!"

"Yeah, I know that. That's why I'm calling you."

"Don't get snippy. I'll see what I can do. Scranton, Charlotte, Binghamton, and Memphis. Something about that combination seems familiar."

"Want me to tell you or are you going to try to guess?"

"No, no. I'll get it in a second."

I hummed the Jeopardy theme. "Thanks, smart ass," he said.

"You're welcome."

"Moonlight Graham!"

"You got it."

Jerry became very excited. "You're looking for a real Moonlight Graham jersey?"

"Yes, but I need it for a trade."

"A trade?"

"Yeah, the client won't sell a jersey I need unless I find him a Moonlight Graham."

"What is the jersey you're swapping for?"

"Eddie Sloane's K.C. jersey."

"What the hell? That's not even close to a fair trade. Who wants an Eddie Sloane Royals jersey?"

"His daughter."

"So, why is the client asking the moon for the Royals jersey? The moon, get it?"

"Funny. He's doing this to be an ass. That's the best way I can explain it."

"Well he may be being an ass, but he's got you being a fool! Unless the client is paying you pretty well."

"This one's personal, but I am getting paid."

"Not well?"

"Not really."

"Is there a woman involved?"

"Maybe."

"Quick, you'll never learn. You'd be a lot less poor if you would just pick one."

"Thanks, Jerry. Can you help me?"

"I'll see what I can do."

A few hours later, Jerry called me back. "I've got some news for you."

"Good or bad?"

"Great news actually. I might have found your jersey."

"Really?"

"Yes, I have a great lead. First, I'm e-mailing you now all the images of the jerseys. But it's the one I don't have that might be the one."

"Go on."

"About seven years ago, we had a special order. We get so many that I had forgotten about this one until I started checking for clues for you. Anyway, a gentleman had researched all the Moonlight Graham jerseys and supplied us with the details, pictures, etc. Usually, it's the other way around, but this guy knew his stuff. So, I'm looking through his file and there was a thank you note. It said 'Now my collection is complete.' He had us make the Scranton, Charlotte, and Memphis jerseys. Not the Binghamton!"

"I'm not sure I'm making the connection."

"You see, I didn't know about Binghamton at the time," Jerry explained. "Normally I would have researched it and found that he was missing Binghamton from his request, but he supplied the research. All we had to do is follow the specifications."

"And so..."

"And so he didn't have us make Binghamton because he already had it! Someone who had done that much research would have surely known that Graham played in all four towns and would have had us make it."

"So you think he only had you make three jerseys instead of four because he had one."

"Exactly."

"I suppose—it's not like anyone else was making replicas, and if they were and he had one, he would have had the other company make the other three. I think you're on to something."

"I think this guy has the Binghamton jersey. The question is, whose jersey is it? Is it truly Moonlight Graham's?"

"So, can you give me the guy's name and number?"

"Yes, and I have even better news."

"What's that?"

"He's in Phoenix."

***

I rang the doorbell and two people came to the door at the home of Jerry's customer. Neither was Martin Cooper. The middle-aged duo were his children, Martha and Sam. They were very skeptical of me and I suppose were there to keep me from swindling their father.

Now at this point, it probably bears reminding that I'm not a criminal or a cheat. I would never take advantage of a guy like Martin Cooper. That's not to say I don't often operate in the gray fringes of the business world, but that it is to be expected when working with antiques and collectibles. There are a lot of dishonest people in this business. One doesn't work around hogs and not get a little muddy from time to time. However, I would never take a man like this. Carl Byrne, in a heartbeat. But not Mr. Cooper.

"Mr. Quick. Welcome!"

Martin was a gracious host, even if his progeny were standoffish. We spent a great deal of time talking baseball and artifacts, alternating with questions from his son and daughter about my intentions.

"I'm here to see the Moonlight Graham jersey. I would like to authenticate it, and if you're open to it, offer a price for it."

"What makes you think we're willing to sell," his daughter asked.

"Your father told me he was open to it."

"Dad," the daughter said, "Why did you say that?"

I asked, "I don't understand. Is it not for sale?"

"Dad doesn't want the jersey in another collector's home," Martha Cooper said.

"I can speak for myself." The old man rose up and beckoned me to follow. We walked down a pleasant hallway, filled with pictures of kids, grandkids, and at least three very large poodles. The poodles weren't photographs—they were live and giving me a low-level snarl. I have no idea why, because I like dogs.

Mr. Cooper opened the door at the end of the hall, revealing a modestly sized man cave. Across the back of the room were four jerseys in frames. The first three were familiar from the pictures Jerry sent me. The fourth was very different. Not just because of the team, but it was clearly older. Worn and washed and worn again. It had been through a full baseball season. There were wrinkles and frays.

I asked permission to approach and look closer. I studied the tags, the stitching, the materials. I studied the fading of the colors, and the hint of a grass stain on the bottom right corner of the shirt. "It's authentic."

"Indeed it is," Martin Cooper said, proudly.

"Any idea which player might have worn it?"

"Well, Moonlight of course."

"It's not that I don't believe you, but it's easy to be taken. They didn't have numbers back then, so there is no way to know from looking at the jersey if this one was his."

"No, they didn't have numbers, but they did have an equipment manager who sewed the names of the players into the insides of the jerseys."

He handed me a picture of the inside, taken before the jersey was framed. Sure enough, sewn in black on the inside of the jersey was "A. Graham."

"It's real," I said.

"And it's not for sale." His daughter had been standing in the doorway. She came in with her brother right behind.

"My father doesn't want to sell the jersey," Martha Cooper repeated.

"It's not that I don't want to sell, Mr. Quick. I told you on the phone that I did. It's just that I would rather see it in a museum than in a private collector's home."

"That's where you've had it all these years."

"I know. It's hypocritical of me, but I feel bad about it being in a place that nobody can see."

"So, where does that leave us?"

The son chimed in. "He needs the money, let him sell it."

"If we were to sell it," Martha asked, "how much could we get?"

"I'm estimating $10,000."

"He needs that money," Sam said.

"But he doesn't want to sell," Martha insisted.

"What if I told you I could get you the money and I could guarantee it would hang in a museum? Would that make everyone happy?"

"I suppose it would," Martha said.

"Just hang on to it and give me 24 hours to get you a check."

"How can you guarantee it will stay in a museum," she asked.

"I need 24 hours on that too."

Chapter Fifteen

On the way back, I called Kevin in Indianapolis to tell him my news and to see if he had had any luck tracking down one himself.

"Technically, I found a Moonlight Graham jersey."

"That's great, I think. Why does the word 'technically' give me a lump in my throat? What's the problem?"

"Well, it's game used, just not the kind of game you were probably thinking of when you told me to look."

"What is it, a football jersey?"

"No, why would you guess that?"

"Moonlight Graham played football at University of Maryland. Believe me, I've thought about venturing out into one of the lesser sports in order to make this Byrne guy happy."

"Well, this is much lesser."

"How much lesser?"

"Church charity softball."

"What?"

"Yeah, the church he attended did a charity softball tournament in 1960."

"He would have been 80 years old by then!"

"Yeah, he didn't play. He was honorary team captain so they made him a jersey and it has his name and a number on the back. I know it's not what you're looking for, but since he played in the era before teams had names and numbers, this might be the only jersey he ever wore with a name and number on the back. That would have some significance, right?"

"Hmm ... this might have to do. What kind of verification provenance do we have?"

"The owner has a photo of Doc Graham wearing the jersey at the local park with the rest of the team."

"What does your gut say?"

"You're the expert, you tell me?"

"Yeah, but I'm trying to train you."

"Could be Photoshopped, but it looks real."

"Did you check with the church to see if anyone has any history of the event?"

"No."

"Did you get a brand on the jersey to make sure it was one being used back then?"

"No."

"Did you ask for pictures to be e-mailed to you, including close-ups showing tags, brand, logos, etc.?"

"No."

Still not crossing all the T's, but he's learning. "Alright, check with the church and get the pictures.

Then forward them to me. If it all checks out, we'll make an offer. Did he give you a price?"

"He's between one thousand and fifteen hundred," Kevin said.

"I doubt it's a fake. One, Chisholm, Minnesota, isn't a hotbed of forgery, and two, if you're going to fake something, you would fake something big. Nobody is faking a church softball jersey."

"Do you think the client is going to buy a Moonlight Graham church softball jersey?"

"Well, when you say it like that, no, not at all." I paused for a second. "That's why I'm not going to say it like that."

"How are you going to say it?"

"With a lot more jam on the bread," I answered. "You let me worry about it. Call me as soon as you hear something, don't make me call you."

"Got it."

I hung up with Kevin and pulled over so I wasn't driving and web surfing. After a few strategic moves on Wikipedia, it was time to mess with a certain bat company owner. I called Byrne's office and his assistant put me through. "Mr. Byrne?"

"Yes?"

"It's Jonathan Quick. I have some news that might interest you."

"Did you find the Moonlight Graham jersey?"

"Well, when one does a search like this, one finds that unexpected things happen."

"Look, I told you that the Moonlight Graham jersey was the only one I would trade for, so if you can't get it, stop wasting my time."

"I assure you that I'm not wasting your time. It's just that my original bargain to you was for a circa 1900s Moonlight Graham jersey in exchange for the Royals jersey."

"Correct."

"Well, I've come across something much more valuable and I feel new terms are warranted."

"What the hell are you talking about?"

"I've located an item that's even more rare than a jersey he played in and I think it's worth more than just an even swap for some retired utility player's jersey."

"You little bastard. If you want that Royals jersey you'll swap me even, that was the deal."

"And if you want the only jersey Moonlight Graham managed semi-pro baseball in, you'll consider my new terms. I bet you didn't even know he had been a manager, did you? You know how to get in touch with me." I hung up on him before he could respond.

Now, you're probably saying that I just lied to the man. No, I just stretched the boundaries of reality ever so slightly. I took the notion of playing for charity (money did still change hands) and stretched it into semi-pro. Of course, I was going to have to make up an entire story around this mythical semi-pro team, but I figured I could piece it together.

In the meantime, he's seething in his office. First, he's pissed as hell that I would have the gumption to renegotiate the deal. He's brokered enough real estate deals to think he is the master of the universe and no autograph hawker (as he called me when we met) is going to get the best of him.

Next, he's going to Google Moonlight Graham and look at the Wikipedia entry for him. There he is going to find the bio that I updated as soon as I got off the phone with Kevin. Sure, some baseball historian will challenge the entry and my update to the article will get scrubbed. Doesn't matter. It only has to stay up there long enough to let Byrne find the paragraph and read that Graham coached semi-pro baseball when he was in his 80s and that a jersey is believed to exist and is highly sought after.

His greed will take over his reason. He will be in a state of combined anguish and envy. He wants this jersey. He can't bear the thought of it not being his. But he can't bear the idea of capitulating to this snot-nosed hustler from Indiana. He's torn. But he has to win. He's type A. He has to come out on top. He will reason that getting the Graham jersey for the Royals jersey and whatever else I want is still a win. It's a win because the Royals jersey is not worth anything and he is so close to a major prize. He thinks a little more, settles it in his mind.

I start to count out loud, "Three, two, one." And the phone rings.

"Mr. Byrne."

"I want that jersey."

"I thought you might."

"What are your terms?"

"The Royals jersey, plus $5,000."

"You're out of your mind!"

"There's a buyer in Scottsdale. I'm ready to make a deal with him today if you're not interested." I knew I had him over a barrel, so I wasn't backing down. Bluffing? Hell yes, I was! But I'm a damn good bluffer.

"Three thousand and the jersey," Byrne countered.

"Done. I'll call you tomorrow to set up a meeting." I hung up on him before he had a chance to think, ask questions, or change his mind. Get the answer you want and get off the phone.

Next I called Kevin. "Did you get all the photos and answers?"

"Yeah, I just e-mailed them to you. It looks legit."

"Great. Offer him a thousand and negotiate up. You should be able to get it for $1,200. If you go over that, I will have to punish you when I get back."

"And if I get it under that?"

"I'll buy the first round."

"You will buy all the rounds."

"Alright, all the rounds. Just make sure that thing gets overnighted here. Pay him a little extra if you have to in order to get it shipped right away."

"Pay her."

"Her?"

"Yeah, it's the former pastor's granddaughter who has the jersey."

"Did she sound cute?"

"She sounded like a pastor's granddaughter."

"Sometimes they are the biggest sinners, if you know what I mean."

"You really need to settle down."

"Why does everyone keep telling me that?"

"Because it's true!"

"Alright, save me the sermon and get that jersey here as soon as possible."

***

Kevin shipped me the Moonlight Graham jersey and FedEx brought it to the hotel. I picked up the box at the front desk and brought it to my room to open. It looked just like a jersey from the '60s should look. I thought the frame looked cheesy, but it would have to do. Byrne would have it reframed anyway, so I didn't care. If this were a normal customer, I would have gone the extra mile by reframing it before bringing it to the customer and working the expense into the price. But I didn't want any repeat business from this guy. Especially since I was going to help ruin his empire in a few days.

When I got to his office, Byrne was in a foul mood. I think he wanted to get back at me for not giving him the last word on the phone. "I've checked into you."

"Yeah, what did you learn?"

"You don't have a pot to piss in, most days. But you do have a house to shit in."

"How's that?"

"I know about your expansive real estate holdings in Maine." He laughed. "Your uncle left you an outhouse."

"He had a sense of humor."

"It seems about right for you. I think you're full of shit. But, I guess that's what makes you able to come up with items like this." He took the box from my hands and set it on the coffee table. Gently, he slid the frame from the box.

He looked at it and nodded. Then he asked me, "Why do you think he's so popular with people?"

"I think it's because people relate to getting close to their dreams and not making it as far as they would have liked. I think they also like the idea that he had an amazing and full life after not getting his major league at-bat."

"I suppose they do. Do you know why I wanted this?"

"Did you have a dream you didn't see fulfilled?"

"No, it's a reminder that I'm a winner. That I've crushed other men's dreams. That if I don't stay a winner, I could someday feel the emptiness he felt for not getting to hit in a Major League game."

"Wow." I wanted to point out that Graham's life was nowhere near empty, but Byrne spoke before I could.

"You're fighting back the urge to call me an asshole aren't you?" He looked at an envelope on the desk. "Afraid I won't give you that check?"

"Yeah, I'll wait to tell you after I deposit it to tell you what I think."

"Coward."

"Why don't you give me the money and the Royals jersey and let's call it a day?"

So, now you're thinking, what's he going to do with the other Moonlight Graham jersey? Good question! There is no way I would want a complete douchebag like Byrne to have a real game-used jersey worn by someone as upstanding as Doc Graham. That's why I was okay with passing this church softball jersey off on him as something with a little more historical significance than it really had. As for the real game-used one, I knew that Charlie Bell of the Fungo Society had deep pockets as well as the respect for history that I had. He could liberate the jersey from Martin Cooper for $10,000 and I knew he would agree to let it be on loan to the Baseball Hall of Fame for a while. I felt confident that I could get the Cooper family to agree to those terms.

Sure, now that I had a deal with Byrne, I didn't need the other jersey. But, some deals I do for the love of the game. I wasn't going to make much (if anything) off this deal, but I knew it meant that the jersey would be in

Cooperstown and that's all that mattered. This thing was special to a lot of people who loved the book and loved the movie. I wanted them to be able to see it and appreciate it.

Charlie Bell was easy. He jumped at the chance to own the jersey and since he spent his summers in upstate New York, he didn't mind it being just an hour away. The family was a bit trickier. They wanted a contract drawn up and to have it signed and notarized. Turning this around was pretty important to me because I wanted out of Phoenix as soon as the Fungos sprang their little St. Patty's Day trick. I didn't want to be in the same state as Byrne when his bat empire came crumbling down and he went looking for someone to blame.

Of course, just when you think you have everything just the way you want it, that's when things start to go awry. What happened next was so bad, I actually used the word awry. And it all happened because of a girl and a baseball, like so many things in life that, like I said, go awry.

Chapter Sixteen

This sordid part of the story began while I was in the hotel bar. It was late evening of same day—a celebration of sorts. I hadn't delivered the jersey to Jessica yet, but I had convinced her to join us at the ballpark for the exploding bat extravaganza. Rainbow excused himself to go to the bathroom. We were talking about pitching along with a variety of other topics and, as usual, I was carrying a baseball. As I waited for Rainbow to return, I practiced various pitch grips and pretended to throw the ball. Then I would take a drink. Then pitch. Then drink.

My hand must have been a little wet from condensation on the glass because I brought my hands up like I was coming to the set position in a pitching windup and the ball just shot out of my hand. It hit the wood floor and rolled across the bar. I followed it as it rolled towards the door and stopped. Stumbling after it, I caught up to it just as it reached the glass doors. I bent down to pick it up and the door opened, sending the ball off in another direction.

"Hey, that was my ball."

"I'm sure you have another one to play with. Most guys have two."

I looked back from where the ball was going to the place it had been when the door opened. In its place were black suede heels, with ankle straps. Attached to the heels were legs that went up and up and up. They were finally met with a dark blue skirt that was cut just shy of obscene. I rose from the ground and stepped out of her way. She was followed by two men in suits who were wearing sunglasses. It was nearly midnight, for heaven's sake.

She sat down at the bar. They took a booth where at least one of them could see everyone coming and going. The other kept his eyes on her.

I approached her with the confidence of a man who had been just crawling at her feet and who had consumed a half bottle of rum.

"I'm not drunk," I said.

"I'm not available," she replied.

Where do you go from there? I'm not the creepy type who won't take no for an answer. But I am the type who will try to end it on a high note.

"I have an idea."

"Oh, really?" Her eyes rolled.

"I'm just going to go get my ball. You stay there and continue to be unavailable."

"I'll do that."

"Oh, and if the CIA-looking dudes who followed you in are unavailable too, my friend here"—Ruben walked up just then—"is going to be very disappointed. He's really into alternative role playing."

This made her crack just the tiniest smile, as if she wanted to laugh but was somehow restrained. "I'm into what," asked Ruben.

"Nothing, let's call it a night." I picked up my baseball and made for the door. As I left, I turned around to see if she was looking. She was. So were the henchmen.

What happened next really was not my fault. Can I be held responsible for the completely biological need of human beings to replenish fluids? Of course not. So it's completely not my fault that at 1 a.m., I was thirsty. Even less my fault that I need ice in my water. I can't drink water without ice. So, I went for a stroll to fill up my bucket and the ice machine had a sign reading, "Out of order, please use the ice machine on floor eight or ten." I was on floor nine. I got on the elevator. When the door opened on floor ten, there was the woman from the bar. The heels were gone, so she was actually shorter than me now. Her short skirt had been replaced by a robe and she was carrying a beach towel.

"I don't think you're going to catch any rays at this hour."

"I'm going for a swim."

"What about the henchmen?"

"They're asleep. This is the only time I get alone."

"Well, then I won't bother you. Good night."

She leaned in and touched my hand. "Go with me."

I looked down and said, "I'm not wearing a swimsuit."

"So go change and meet me at the pool."

Some orders must be obeyed. When a strange, beautiful woman tells me to meet her at the pool at nearly midnight, those orders must be carried out to the letter.

Ten minutes later I was in the pool and not asking questions. Neither was she. We didn't swim any laps, but we did get a hell of a workout. After the pool, we went to the hot tub. I've always thought hotel hot tubs were gross because of the things you imagined people do in them. That is until I found myself doing the things that I imagined people doing in them. I didn't find doing it gross at all. In fact, it was quite pleasant. I would have been happy to repeat the whole thing the following evening if it wasn't for the henchmen. Why on earth would I get involved with a woman who has henchmen? Maybe Kevin is right. Maybe I should settle down.

At this point, I feel the need to give you some dating advice. Women with henchmen have them for one of two reasons: there is a jealous overprotective boyfriend/ husband somewhere or there is something about them that attracts danger. This could be wealth, power, and/ or beauty. Regardless of the reason, you are taking a huge risk getting involved with a woman who has henchmen watching over her. I recommend ferreting out this information about a woman early in the conversation.

She may simply refer to them as bodyguards (the more politically correct term) but they're still henchmen and you should beware of trouble.

In this case, the woman had a jealous fiancé, a fact she chose to disclose that morning when I suggested breakfast.

"I think we should order room service."

"That wouldn't be wise," she replied.

"Watching your figure?"

"No, but my boyfriend's men are watching it."

"Excuse me?"

"My boyfriend. My fiancé. His men are always watching me. I'm like a prisoner," she added.

"Were they watching last night?"

"Of course not. Why do you think I went swimming at midnight?"

"Is it safe to assume that you and your boyfriend…"

"Fiancé," she corrected me.

"Fiancé, right. Yes, there's that word that didn't seem to make it into the discussion last night."

"Are you worried? Are you a scared little boy or are you a man?"

"I'm pretty sure I'm a man," I answered. "I was when we finally fell asleep, anyway. However, I'm just trying to get a sense of what I'm dealing with here. For example, why does your fiancé have men following you?"

"He's says it's for my safety, so a rival gang doesn't kidnap me to get to him. I think he's full of the shit." Her English was a little off. I guess I didn't notice so much last night. But, we were naked and I make it a point to never critique the grammar of naked women.

"Rival gang. Kidnapping. Henchmen. What exactly does your fiancé do for a living?"

"He deals in narcotics," she answered matter of factly. Shrugging, she added, "And he has a chain of appliance stores. But mostly he deals drugs."

My legs went numb. I sat back on the bed and pondered my fate. "Jealous man, your fiancé?"

She licked her lips. "Very jealous. He most likely will have you killed." This seemed to delight her for some reason.

I grabbed my pants. "That's why we're going to keep this between you and me. What happens in Camelback stays in Camelback, right?"

"Don't you want to fight for me, Mr. Baseball Man?"

She was the second woman that called me baseball man. Even though Mr. Baseball Man probably was meant to be a put-down from her, it sounded sexy in her accent. Plus, she was still naked under the covers, so that might have had something to do with it.

"I do want to fight for you. But against minor leaguers. Not pros! I'm used to rednecks and insurance salesmen— not drug kingpins who order other men to kill people. Speaking of which, just where are the henchmen?"

"Who are these henchmen you speak of?"

"Your fiancé's men. The ones who are watching you."

"They're next door."

"Really?" I looked at the wall between our rooms. "Really? So last night, did you just go looking for a swim and a guy to have killed? Is this what you do for fun?"

"Was it not fun?" She pulled the sheet off to reveal her body. "Don't you think I'm worth it?"

I hesitated. "Yeah...no. No. NO! Not getting killed."

"Keep your voice down. They will hear you and know I have a man in my room." Of course there was a knock at the door that instant.

"Maria, open up."

"Turn on the TV and get in the shower."

I grabbed my clothes and the remote. I hit the on button and darted into the bathroom. Maria moved to the door and I slid into the shower.

"Are you alone?"

"Of course," Maria told the henchman in the hall.

"I heard voices."

"Maybe you are a crazy man. Maybe I should tell my fiancé you hear voices." Now she didn't sound sexy. She sounded mean.

"Just hurry up and get ready. Antonio is picking you up at 11:30."

"Alright, alright." She shut the door, moved across the room and came into the bathroom. "What is my naughty baseball man doing?"

"I was thinking of going to confession."

"Are you Catholic?"

"No, but I think it might be a good idea, given I spent the night with a drug lord's girlfriend."

"Fiancé."

"Fiancé, right."

"Well, you can't go to confession yet."

"Why?"

"I haven't finished sinning with you." She dropped her robe and tried to get into the shower with me.

"No, really, I've got to go."

"You're not going anywhere. If you want to live through this, your best bet is to stay hidden in here until I leave with them. Then head back to your room. They won't come back in here."

You have to hand it to her, she had a good plan. And I was happy to stay put in the shower, wash her back, and whatever else needed it.

At 11:20, Maria was dressed and ready to go. "Goodbye Mr. Baseball Man. I hope you find the green bat."

My heart sunk into my stomach. Had I, in a moment of weakness and wetness, given away the plan to sabotage Byrne Bats? "Did I talk in my sleep?"

"You said you had to find the green bat. Why the green bat? Is it worth a lot of pesos?"

"Yes, many pesos. You should forget about that now. And forget about Mr. Baseball Man."

She caressed my cheek. "I could never forget about you. Are you sure you don't want to fight my fiancé for me? It would make my afternoon much more entertaining."

"I'm pretty sure."

"You are a coward."

"You say coward, I say pragmatic."

"Pragmatic? You mean you sleep with the boys and the girls?"

"No, no! Pragmatic means logical. Sensible."

"Scared."

"Yes, scared."

"Goodbye Mr. Baseball." She gave me a long tongue-filled goodbye kiss. It had the intensity and moisture of our time in the hot tub, with fewer towels needed afterwards. Then she sprang from the bed, grabbed her bag and marched out the door. I could hear her talking to the henchmen as she left. I waited about five minutes and checked the peephole. Nobody in sight. I opened the door and there was a henchman coming back to the room.

We exchanged an awkward moment of silence. Then he hit me so hard, my underwear fell off.

***

When I awoke, my underwear was indeed off. I assume it was from the punch, but I could have just as easily been stripped naked by the henchmen. It's just hard to imagine a hit so hard it knocked me unconscious would not have the power to jolt undergarments from their intended spot.

As I came to, I took note of my surroundings. The room was filled with smoke and cardboard boxes—some stacked on shelves and some scattered about. Just the sort of place that a drug lord would use to store drugs, guns, and dead bodies. At least that was my first impression. As I sat there longer and adjusted to the light, it looked a lot less evil. In fact, it looked like the warehouse of an appliance store. Boxes and boxes of refrigerators, washers, dryers, and dishwashers.

Initially, I thought the smoke came from workers or henchmen having a cigarette break. Then my nose caught up with the rest of my senses. Something was burning and it smelled like someone was cooking tuna with a blowtorch.

"Dammit Harry, you left the hot plate on again. You're going to burn this place down and Mr. Beasley is going to sue you!"

Mr. Beasley? I thought this place was owned by a Mexican drug lord. Since when are Mexicans named Beasley? I listened as the conversation got closer. When they got real close, things got weird.

"Harry, when you were back here trying to toast your tuna sandwich, did you happen to tie up a naked man?"

"Can't say that I did, Mr. Otto. Why do you ask?"

"Because there's a naked man tied up back here," answered Mr. Otto.

"Good morning," I started.

"It's afternoon."

"I stand corrected. Good afternoon."

"That remains to be seen. Can't say that finding a naked man was ever the start of a good afternoon. Can you, Harry?"

"No," Harry replied. Naked woman maybe. But not a naked man."

"Of course. Naked woman presents a whole other set of circumstances. But a naked man, now that's a problem." Mr. Otto glared at me.

"I don't want to be a problem," I said.

"But you see, you are a problem. You're not where you're supposed to be and you're naked. By my calculation, that's two problems."

"If you could just let me go, I could stop being a problem."

"Now, that presents another problem. How do I know you weren't causing even more problems free and naked? How do I know you weren't tied up in order to curtail the problem?"

"I wasn't curtailed. I was hit by a henchman."

He thought for a moment. "Very curious. You buy that, Harry?"

"Not really," Harry answered. "Henchmen don't usually take people's clothes off."

"No, they don't." Mr. Otto turned to me, "Why are you naked?"

"When I woke up, my clothes were gone."

"Your clothes were gone and you're naked in this warehouse. Where were you when you got hit?"

"In a hotel."

"Were you perhaps, fornicating?"

"At the time of the punch, no."

Mr. Otto continued, "Had you been fornicating prior to the punch?"

"How much prior?"

He raised his voice, "Mr. Naked Man in the warehouse, in the hours leading up to you being knocked out and winding up here, did you or did you not fornicate?"

"Only a few times."

"A few times. Isn't that something, Harry? Here sits a man tied up and naked because he was out fornicating. Should we let such a man free? Don't you suppose someone had a good reason to tie this man up?"

"I'm sure they had a good reason," Harry said.

"Harry thinks you're here for a reason. So do I."

"Fellas, we can talk about this?"

"Harry, let's let this man sit and contemplate what must be an abundance of errors of his ways."

"Fellas! Seriously, come back and untie me." Nothing. They left me tied to that chair. I guess it could have been worse. I guess they could have killed me. However, somebody tied me up and put me here? Who?

"He's back here boss." I recognized the cologne of the henchman. I could hear the footsteps of three men approaching. Henchman number one, henchmen number two, and Tony Beasley. Tony Beasley!

In perfect unison, Tony and I both said, "What the hell are you doing here?"

"You're the drug lord?"

"You're the guy who slept with Maria?"

"You're cheating on your wife!"

"Well you're sleeping with my girlfriend. You're my memorabilia guy!" For many years I had helped Tony sell and buy a variety of artifacts. Tony is a successful businessman, but a somewhat insecure one, which explained the occasional splashy sports memorabilia purchase. I wasn't sure what explained all of this behavior.

"You're not a drug lord, are you?"

"Untie him and give him his clothes. No, but it gets her off thinking I'm a criminal."

"Seriously? You're cheating on your wife and pretending to be a drug lord? You're going to get yourself killed!"

"Me? My guys might have killed you."

"Really, murder? That's not your style."

"No, not really. But when I heard she was two-timing me, I was pretty pissed. Can't believe she was nailing you."

"If it makes you feel any better, it was just one night."

"Not really, but thanks."

"What are you doing, Tony? She's half your age. Do you love her?"

"No, I guess I just love the idea of her."

"Well, she thinks she's going to marry you. Where did she get that idea?"

"Oh, she knows I'm not leaving my wife. She just likes the rush she gets by pretending to be engaged to a drug lord. Apparently her brother is a real drug dealer and she thinks he's Superman."

"Tony, this is the most dysfunctional tryst I've ever heard of."

"Really, you're lecturing me?"

"But one of you is going to wind up dead. You both keep throwing around that drug lord story and a real gang is going to think you're muscling in on their turf. Or worse, the FBI is going to come crashing in and arrest you on suspicion of narcotics trafficking."

Which was exactly what happened next. Glass broke behind us and tear gas canisters bounced across the floor. The double overhead garage doors were thrown open and FBI and Drug Enforcement Administration agents swarmed the place. Do you have any idea how hard it is to wipe your eyes when you're tied to a chair? Do you know how awkward it is to try to explain to shouting DEA agents that you've been tied to a chair naked by mistake?

It was humiliating. Mostly because as the chaos subsided and everyone was being booked and interviewed, nobody untied me. It was like they were making me go last on purpose. "Can I get a towel?" Nothing.

"Maybe a jacket or something."

Still being ignored.

Finally I shouted, "You know I don't have on any sunscreen and the afternoon sun is right on my penis!"

That got me a towel across the lap. At least I was protected from the harmful rays of the sun.

Chapter Seventeen

The Phoenix police were very understanding, which is to say that they gave me a towel, took me to jail with the rest of the group and made me wait for two hours before I was questioned. The bigger fish were being fried so I was left to wait in a holding cell with three college students who had been selling marijuana and a barista who had lost it on the 1,498th person who had used the word expresso instead of espresso. In other words, I was extremely glad not to be with a group of hardened criminals, being a newbie to this. I was however, dying to get out and watch the YouTube video of the barista.

Ruben picked me up and lectured me all the way to the hotel. Ramona scowled at me as I walked into the lobby. There was no getting past her. I had no room key. I had to approach the desk. She lit into me in Spanish for a good five minutes. She had seen the hotel video of the pool shenanigans. I was certain she was about to kick me out of the hotel, when she noticed someone come up behind me. She activated a new key and handed it across the counter. "Here is your new key, Mr. Quick."

I turned around and there was Mrs. Middle America again. She just shook her head. I didn't have any clever words to say. I just hung my head and walked to the elevator. I would have liked to check out the next day, but the bats were coming and we had our work cut out for us. I knew I deserved Ramona's anger and I resolved to make it up to her. The problem was, I was only scratching the surface of how much trouble this Maria incident was going to be.

***

Phillip Jones struck me as an angry man. He got off the plane angry. He made his way to the baggage claim angry. He waited angry. There was anger in the way he yanked the large black duffel off the beltway. There was anger in the way he pushed through the crowd to get to ground transportation. I was at the airport to make sure he got there and to make sure our courier made the pickup.

The airport was busy with spring breakers shuffling their families here and there, trying to flag cabs and hotel shuttles. It was a perfect environment to blend in—to observe and not be observed. Right on time, a black limousine approached the loading zone. Phillip approached and a window went down. He got down on one knee and unzipped the black duffel. Reaching in, he gently pulled out a long, slender box. He removed the tape from the top and started to pull out an object.

"Hurry up, you," yelled a cop. "Keep it moving."

Phillip nodded in acknowledgment and turned back to the box. He pulled out a bright green bat and handed it to an outstretched arm from the limo. A minute later, the bat came back. Phillip put it back into the box and then slid it into the duffel. Just then a white van pulled in front of the limo. A driver got out and walked towards Phillip. He pushed a clipboard towards him and he signed it. The driver acknowledged the signature and nodded his head towards the limo. Then he took the bag, put it in the back of the van and beckoned to Philip to get in. They pulled away and the window of the limo went up. The limo pulled out while the van waited, and then the van pulled out. It was at this point that I noticed a blue Buick that pulled out behind the van. I had heard the cop yelling at the Buick driver.

This could be a problem. They were being followed. I sent a text to the van driver. We had agreed that nobody would contact Phillip so no messages could be traced back to him. The driver might not be able to see my text until he stopped. I wanted to make sure he didn't open the back wide enough for anyone to see that there were two black duffels in the back of the van.

I didn't think I should follow them, so I headed to George's workshop to wait. Nearly three hours later, the white van pulled up. "Any trouble?"

"No, but I did spot the tail, even before I saw your text. Pretty lousy job of following if they didn't want me to know they were there."

"How did it go at the MLB office?"

"Fine. I escorted Mr. Jones and the bats inside. I had to sit in the lobby while they did the weighing and measuring and then we packed up and went to the hotel."

"And did the Buick follow all the way?"

"Yes, and they never really tried to be inconspicuous."

"Maybe that was the point. Maybe Byrne wanted to scare you before you thought of doing something devious."

"You mean like this?" He handed me the bag with the bats.

I opened them and pulled out a bat from the open box. It was beautiful. The green might be a little garish to some people, but I did admire the construction. Seemed a shame to destroy it, but it had to be done. George rushed up, perturbed. "Christ, we don't have time to stand around admiring the damn things! We've got to get to work!"

He and his nephew scooped up the duffel and made for the workshop. Various stations had been set up for the variety of tasks that were needed to pull this off. Tommy was good with a lathe, so he began sanding the finish off the bats. George's nephew then cut the bats in two pieces, with the cut coming about four inches from the top of the bat. He then bored holes in both pieces about an inch in diameter. George would then pack them with an air canister, a spring mechanism, and the packed confetti. The idea was for the contact with the ball to crack the bat and trip the spring, which would deploy the air canister. The blast of air would launch the top of the bat with a trail of Irish-themed confetti behind it. Spectacular.

"Did anyone try this with another bat to see if it would actually work?"

I looked at George. George looked at Rainbow. Rainbow looked at Scooter. "Not that I'm aware of," Rainbow answered.

Scooter argued, "Are you guys kidding me? We're going to risk going to jail and you don't even know if this will work?"

"Will it work, George?" I asked.

"It will work."

I looked back at Scooter, "George says it will work."

"Well, la-di-frickin-da! George says it will work. Does George know baseball bats?"

"George knows wood, better than anyone I know. And in case you've forgotten, bats are made of wood." I replied.

Scooter looked at George. "You think it will work?"

"It will work," George repeated.

Scooter turned around and walked back outside. "No worries. George says it will work."

After packing the bats, George put wood putty on the line that formed when the two pieces were rejoined. Then he sanded and coated them with his own special sealer. I asked, but he wouldn't tell me what was in it. Finally, he applied the paint. He used a type of oven to dry the paint quickly. These wouldn't have as good a finish as a normal bat would have. But we only needed them to look good enough to be used in one at-bat.

"What if one of these guys takes a cut during batting practice? Won't we be done for?"

"No, they signed a deal that the bats have to be used first in the first at-bat. Byrne didn't want any nicks or smudges to the finish since all eyes would be on them."

"What if the canister doesn't go off?"

"It will go off, don't worry!"

Around 1 a.m. I began to worry. The sanding process was completely finished. All the bats had been cut but George had about 12 left to pack. His nephew was applying putty, but George had to sign off on each one before he would approve it. Sanding, cutting, packing, putty, two coats of paint. Flash dry, and a coat of lacquer. I didn't see how we were going to do it. This was going to be close.

I started to listen to the Fungos tell stories to take my mind off it. I couldn't believe they were all still awake.

"You're stuffing those bats with green, orange and white confetti?" Tommy asked.

"Yeah, they're the colors of the Irish flag," replied Hank.

"Nice touch."

"I thought so."

Hal asked, "Do you really think this will work?"

"I don't know. But it's been a helluva ride. Most fun I've had since the '77 playoffs," said Tommy.

"You were still playing in '77," I asked.

"I was coming out of the pen."

Hal jumped in, "You were washed up in '77."

Hank defended Tommy. "Aahh, what do you know from washed up? You were already out of the game and trying to open a disco club in '77."

"I miss disco," said Frank.

Everyone looked at him. "What? I do. It was great music."

At 3 a.m., there were twenty finished bats. We had had just three and a half hours left and ten bats to go. I started to get really worried. Rainbow started to panic. But through it all, George just kept working. It was like watching Michelangelo paint the Sistine Chapel. Well, how I imagined he would paint it. No fuss. No panic. Just calmly listening to everyone panic around him and quietly and deliberately calming their fears. He just kept working.

At 6:15, the last bat went into its box. We had fifteen minutes to spare in case traffic got weird. The courier pulled up shortly thereafter and we loaded up the bats. I followed them out of the industrial park and out towards Peoria. The courier drove to the hotel and Phillip brought the decoy duffel out and helped load it into the truck. Just like at the airport, the Buick was waiting and watching. When the courier pulled out, the Buick followed. I was pretty certain this wasn't a third party but one of Byrne's men making sure the bats got to where they needed to go. I decided to go inside and get a little sleep before the big show.

Chapter Eighteen

On March 17, the Irish world and the wannabe Irish celebrate St. Patrick's Day. One of the traditions passed down about the great St. Patrick was that he drove all the snakes out of Ireland. Today, on the anniversary of his mid-fifth century demise (or sixth, depending on which scholar you believe), we were going to drive a snake out of Phoenix.

For this thing to work, we couldn't let Byrne near his bats. He might spot that something was off. George had done an amazing job of painting and stamping the bats to look they did when they left the factory. But they were still Byrne's and he might spot something the old craftsman had missed.

So, we had come up with a plan to keep Byrne out of the clubhouse before the game. One piece of info we paid dearly for was which stadium he was going to be at for St. Patrick's Day. Our mole had let us know that he planned to do a pre-game photo shoot with the original bat prototype and several of the Dodgers, Tommy

Lasorda and other stars. The photo shoot was taking place at one of the practice diamonds on the backside of the Camelback Ranch complex, in order to have fewer fans hanging about.

After the photo shoot, Byrne was scheduled to make his way to the main field for the game. He planned to go to the clubhouse and take a picture with the Dodgers player who was leading off that day. They were playing the White Sox and since the two teams share the complex, that day the Sox were considered the home team. The Dodgers would bat first.

When the pre-game photo shoot ended, Scooter's lady friend Loretta positioned her golf cart to be the one Byrne took back to the stadium. He smiled and hopped in the back. The Prophet and I waited off in the distance out of sight. When the golf cart pulled out, we followed behind in another cart. As Loretta made her way between the fields, she came up behind two old men walking slowly. One buckled at the knees as they pulled alongside.

His companion grabbed his friend's shoulder and beckoned for help. He looked frantic. We made our way around them, keeping far to their left. We kept on going but the Prophet gave me the play-by-play.

"Loretta is trying to get Byrne to help her get the Hal in the cart."

"What's Hank doing?"

"He's trying to direct them with his cane. Byrne is just acting perturbed and not helping."

"Prick." He looked at me and back at the scene. I apologized, "Sorry, Prophet."

"That's okay. God knows he's a prick."

I pulled the cart to a place where we could both observe. Sure enough, Hank and Loretta were trying to get Hal into the cart. When they finally did, an argument seemed to be arising between Loretta and Byrne. He was yelling and pointing towards the main stadium. She was pointing towards the parking lot.

Loretta won. She charged off towards the parking lot and to where she knew a medic would be waiting next to an ambulance. Byrne continued to argue. As they went by, Byrne caught a glimpse of us and tried to get her attention to stop. She wouldn't have it. We pulled out and made our way to the main stadium.

Rainbow called me on the walkie-talkie. "How's it looking out there?"

"He's off to the main parking lot with Loretta and the boys. I figure they can stall him for another 10 minutes, tops. How are we doing on your end?"

"Good. Wally convinced Ramon that he needed to be on the field early for pictures with the Leprechaun Queen." Ramon Fernandez would be the Dodger leading off the game. Our plan was to keep Byrne and Ramon separate as long as possible so Byrne couldn't take too close a look at that bat.

"The Leprechaun Queen? Who is the Leprechaun Queen?"

"How the hell should I know? You know how superstitious some ballplayers are. I told him that on St. Patrick's Day, the leadoff hitter must kiss the cheek of the Leprechaun Queen or he won't get a hit until April."

"And what's he going to do when he can't find the Leprechaun Queen? He will lose his mind!"

"No no, I got that covered, too. Jessica is sitting in the front row in a bright green dress. Wally's going to escort him over to give her a peck on the cheek."

"Lucky bastard."

Rainbow responded, "He's about to have the most memorable at-bat of his career and it's going to be a disaster. We owe him a kiss from a pretty girl."

"Wait, you said he had to kiss her on the cheek. Not that she had to kiss back."

"It's only courteous to kiss back. Why, are you jealous?"

"No, of course not."

"You haven't been fooling around with her, too, have you?"

I looked at the Prophet. "Let's get back to matter at hand."

"So, we've got it covered in about five minutes. So, if you can keep Byrne out ..."

I cut him off. "He's on his way. He's in a different golf cart and flying towards the stadium. Get Ramon and his green bat out of that clubhouse!"

We followed Byrne as quickly as we could and I tried to radio Wally. "Wally, are you there?"

"I'm here boss, what's up?"

"He's coming! Get Ramon out of there."

"He's tying his shoes and his jersey is still unbuttoned."

"Tie his shoes for him."

"He's a grown man! Besides, I think he can hear you!"

"He doesn't speak English, remember. That's why you're there!"

"Look, I don't think..."

"Dammit Wally!" I paused and looked at Prophet, "Sorry Prophet. Dammit Wally, if Byrne walks in that dugout we're busted! This whole thing comes crashing down."

I waited for a response. Nothing. I started to speak again and heard a voice say, "Ramon! We are so proud to have you on board with Byrne Bats." Then the voice of an interpreter repeating those words in Spanish. Wally had kept the radio on so I would know that Byrne was in the clubhouse. He was sure to see that bat.

I felt a lump in my throat. If he saw that the bats had been tampered with, he could easily have his people call all the teams and pull the bats from use. Maybe he wouldn't think all the bats were bad? Who was I kidding? We were sunk.

"Let's go find Jessica, I told the Prophet.

We made our way into the stadium and into our seats. I was too sick to even order a beer. Jessica could tell from the look on my face that something was wrong.

"What happened?"

"Byrne is in the clubhouse."

"Did he inspect the bat?"

"I'm sure he did."

"But you don't know for sure he found anything, right?"

"I suppose. But this is not good. Not good at all."

"You had enough faith in George to fly him all the way out here. Don't doubt him now."

"I know, but he usually has more than one night to create a masterpiece."

Players began to take the field to warm up. We waited as players walked by. No Ramon. Finally we could hear a man talking in Spanish in the dugout. He was loud and seemed upset. Ramon peeked out from the dugout and scanned the crowd. Although we were right behind him, he was looking away from us. He panned the whole crowd turning slowly until he fixed his gaze on us. The bat he was holding was black.

Suddenly, he started yelling in Spanish and pointing at Jessica. I had a very uneasy feeling as he approached the wall that separates the fans from the field. Behind him stepped a coach in uniform. He interpreted for us. "You are the ones," Ramon said.

I got that lump in my throat back. We were busted. "No, I mean, she is the one."

He looked at Jessica. "She is the Leprechaun Queen," Ramon said through the coach.

"Well of course she is," I answered and pushed Jessica towards the wall. "Kiss him, now," I ordered her via a whisper.

Jessica leaned over the wall and Ramon kissed her cheek. She returned the favor and he marched off to home plate to get in a couple of swings. Although my heart slowed down a little bit, I was still worried because there was no green bat. Of course, he couldn't use it in batting practice per the agreement, but I was worried. Wally wasn't answering his radio, so we were going to be in suspense for a while.

I usually enjoy getting to a park early and watching all the pregame activities. First there is batting practice, then the grounds crew goes to work painting the lines. The game day crew gets ready for the various promotions, people are led onto the field to throw out the first pitch. Performers getting loose for the national anthem. Normally, I'm in heaven awaiting the first pitch. Today, I was in hell! It was torment counting the minutes.

More calls to Wally. No response each time. Finally, the anthem was over and the color guard made its way off the field. And Ramon emerged. He had two bats in his hand, one with a weight. Neither was green. My heart sank. He took two swings with the two black bats, then dropped them both.

A batboy stepped up from the dugout and handed him a new bat. A bright, shiny, new green bat. Whatever had happened in that clubhouse, Byrne had not pulled the bats. We were a go! Ramon was about to get the shock of his life.

Just then texts started coming in from the guys at other ballparks. Green bat. Green bat. Green bat. We had made it this far. The Fungo Society was actually going to pull this off! Well, not so fast. The springs inside the bats still had to work.

Ramon stepped into the box. The pitcher wound up and threw the first pitch in the dirt. Ball one. His next pitch was a little outside. Ramon held off. Ball two. The third pitch was over the plate but a little high. Ramon swung and missed. My heart went into my stomach again! Two balls, one strike. Pitch number four was outside and in the dirt again. Three balls, one strike. Pitch number five was a curveball that hung up just a little too long. Ramon saw a pitch he could drive a mile and swung with all his might.

What happened next will be talked about in bars and around baseball gatherings for years to come. It was a singular moment in the history of the game. Okay, technically it did happen in eight parks at roughly the same time, but it never happened in the game before and will probably never happen again.

Ramon hit the ball and his bat exploded into a green, orange, and white paper shower. The confetti cloud enveloped batter, catcher, and umpire. The spring had worked. George's craftsmanship and ingenuity had come through. Byrne bats had just exploded on highly-promoted livestream Webcasts and in eight different ballparks. I heard Byrne cursing from the luxury suite all the way down to our front row seats. Fans were yelling. Players were examining the damage to the bat. Ramon was as puzzled as anyone. We got up, one by one so as not to draw attention. Most people were focused on the circus at home plate.

On my way out, I noticed the Mine Bats guys sitting in the last row of our section. "Good day for baseball, gentlemen," I told them.

"Did you see that?"

"Yes, I did. Hope the three of you got some rest last night. You're about to get a whole lot of orders." I winked and walked towards the exit.

I told the Fungos I would catch them later and followed Jessica to her car.

"Well, Mr. Quick, that was very satisfying. Highly illegal, but very satisfying."

"I'm glad you approve."

"I must say, when you told me you were going to take those old geezers and turn them into a criminal gang, I thought you were crazy."

"Well, your dad was one of those geezers. What do you think now?"

She grabbed my shirt and pulled me in for a kiss. "I still think you're crazy. But you do know how to get things done."

It's hard to properly thank someone for a compliment when her tongue is in your mouth. What should I do? Should I end the kiss and engage in proper etiquette or just file the thank-you away for later? I decided etiquette could wait.

"It's my lucky day. I've never kissed the Leprechaun Queen before."

"I've never been the Leprechaun Queen before."

"Any chance the Leprechaun Queen would like to have dinner, maybe some green beer, perhaps a frolic under a rainbow?"

"Sorry, that kiss is all the luck I have to share with you today. I have to get back to work. Any chance you can bring my father's jersey by tomorrow?"

"Sure, text me the address." I waved goodbye and wondered how much fun it might have been to spend the rest of the day with the Leprechaun Queen. Then reality set in and I decided it probably would be best to get some distance between me and everything that had happened these past few weeks. My plan was to get out of town before the dust settled. Unfortunately, this is the desert. And there's a lot of dust to go around.

Chapter Nineteen

I was feeling pretty good about acquiring the Royals jersey and the Moonlight Graham one as well. I even felt pretty good about sticking it to Byrne, although I had a nervous feeling a uniformed official was going to question me any minute. I'm not sure if it was rational, but I just felt like if I could get back to Indiana, everything would be fine. However, I did have to resolve things with Ramona because she was working when I got back to the hotel.

My plan was simply to get the jerseys out of her locked office (they were too big for the safe), but she refused until I had heart-to-heart with her. I hadn't kept them in my room because I trusted Ramona more than I did housekeeping. I have to admit how much of a jerk I am by telling you this: my plan was to stall her, get the jerseys and leave town without the little chat. Cowardly and cruel, I know. The shame is welling up in me just recounting it. But we don't always live up to the bar we set for ourselves, do we? Sometimes the moral compass experiences magnetic interference.

But there would be no such cowardly avoidance tonight. Not if I wanted those two jerseys, anyway. Into the business office we went, which was unoccupied. She started yelling and screaming in Spanish. She even slapped me once. I still don't know why. After about five minutes she paused and waited for me to respond.

"Well?"

"Well, what?"

"Well, do you love the whore with the legs?"

"Which whore?"

"There's more than one?" Slap. Screaming in Spanish. Crying. More screaming.

"Who is it going to be? Me or her?"

"Ramona, we just met. I really like you, but you've got to slow down. It's only been a few weeks. It's not like I live here, I'm a guest in your hotel! It's not like we're in a relationship."

"You are a pig. You sleep with me then you want to dump me." Several more words in Spanish.

"Ramona," I said. "We're still getting to know each other." I was scared to death of her by now. "I'm not kicking you to the curb. But be realistic. I have to leave when this business is over. Plus, if we are going to have a relationship, then you can't get jealous when I have a female client. My clients pay the bills."

"A relationship?" she looked me in the eyes. "I knew my baseball man couldn't possibly love the whore with the legs." She started kissing me on the cheeks, the nose, the neck. "I knew my baseball man loved me."

She pulled her hair down and pushed me onto a table. Twenty minutes later we emerged from the office. Just outside the door, wouldn't you know it, was Mrs. Middle America. Ramona came out first, tucking her shirt back in as she walked. Mrs. Middle America looked at her and then looked me up and down. "It's okay," I said to her. "We were just discussing the whore with the legs." She gasped and walked quickly out of the lobby.

Early the next morning, I had breakfast with Charlie Bell, who had picked up the Moonlight Graham jersey so we could complete the deal with the Cooper family. After saying our goodbyes, I grabbed a luggage cart and brought it to my room. With all that had gone on, I had never had time to really study the case holding Eddie's Royals jersey until now. I realized, that although this was a pretty good replica of the craftsmanship of George's case, it wasn't the one he built. It was very similar, but much thicker. On the back, the word "prototype" was written and the Byrne shamrock was stamped below. This must have been the model for his new jersey case line. I wondered if Byrne had put Eddie's jersey in this case after he bought it at auction or if Eddie had come into possession of it. As I studied it more, I realized that based on the photo from the auction house and the light blue fabric I was now looking at, it must have been Eddie who made the switch.

I finished packing and loaded my bags and the jersey onto the cart. When I got to the elevator, the doors opened before I could hit the button. Two very large men dressed in black stepped off, with one holding the elevator door so it wouldn't shut. "Please, push your cart onto the elevator, Mr. Quick."

"Thanks," I replied. Then I asked, "Do I know you?"

"No, but our employer would very much like to have a conversation with you," he responded. The second gentleman unbuttoned his blazer, just enough for me to see the gun holstered inside. "We insist."

I pushed the cart onto the elevator. I didn't ask any questions on the way down and they didn't speak. When the door opened, the first man stepped off and the second waited for me to push the cart and followed behind me. As we moved through the lobby, I spoke up.

"Just let me drop these things off and I'll be right with you fellows."

"The picture comes with us."

"It's just a jersey, not a picture and I don't think we need to bring it with us. It's bulky and will just slow us down."

"Is it valuable?"

"No, just a family memento, nothing you would be interested in."

The other guy wasn't having it. "It comes with us. Not another word." He showed a gun as well.

"Why don't we bring it for show and tell?" I asked. He hit me in the kidney.

I followed quietly, pushing the cart all the way out of the lobby and into the parking lot. Past a long row of cars to the far end of the lot. When we got to their van, the goon with the keys started cursing. "Would you look at this bullshit?"

The car next to him had parked within inches of his door. He moved around to the passenger side and the car on the right had backed in and parked within inches of that side.

"Well, it looks like you fellows have some more pressing issues to deal with," I tried. "How about I just go back in and you call me when you're ready to leave." I started to roll the cart back to the hotel and one of the goons punched me in the other kidney.

"We'll go in through the back."

"Doesn't seem very ladylike," I said, holding my back.

"You're not a lady." I winked at goon two and he hit me with the butt of his gun. As I passed out, I felt the blood trickle down my scalp and wondered why doesn't anyone have a sense of humor anymore.

When I woke up, I was strapped to a wooden chair. In front of me were sand, one large cactus and rocks. About a mile away, I could see a mountain. To my right were more cactuses, a man holding a pipe, and the van. To my left was another guy tied to a chair. He was slumped over, so I couldn't tell who he was. Goon number two came from behind us and splashed water on my kidnap buddy.

He sputtered and spit. Gasped and said a few bad words. I looked at him again and knew exactly who it was. Tony Beasley. At this point a Latino man wearing a very expensive suit stepped in front of us. It was the same man I had seen at the memorabilia show shaking hands with Carl Byrne and kissing Valerie Westergren on the cheek. It was Carlos Gomez. Small world. It was about to get smaller.

He asked, "Which one of you pigs is sleeping with my sister?"

We both looked at each other. He slapped us both. "Who is it?"

"Sir, I don't know what you're talking about," I said. "Who is your sister?"

I heard a car door open and the voice of a woman arguing. The arguing turned into a struggle as it became apparent she wasn't getting out of the car without a fight. After a few minutes, more came into view. Goon number two was pulling on the arm of Maria.

"Which one of you is sleeping with my sister?"

I nudged towards Tony. He did the same to me. "Which one?"

We both did it again. It sank in and his eyes widened. He looked at Maria, "Both of them?"

She smiled sheepishly. "Put her back in the car."

Gomez motioned for someone standing behind us to come forward. The goon handed him a machete, which Gomez instantly put right against my crotch. "I should cut off your testicles and stuff them in your mouth."

He then pressed it against Tony's neck. "And you are a married man. I should cut off your head. You have no honor."

"You're a drug dealer, for crying out loud," Tony said. That got him a punch in the face.

"How I earn my living has nothing to do with my honor. I simply provide a product that the public desires. It is no different that whiskey or toilet paper."

"Except I can't go to jail for wiping my ass." That got me a punch in the face.

"Silence. In my personal affairs I conduct myself with honor. I would never sleep with a man's wife, or defile the purity of a man's sister."

I thought long and hard about pointing out just how unpure his sister was. I can't remember a naughtier woman in the bedroom, knowledge she had learned long before I ever decided to make a trip to Phoenix. However, considering how bad my head hurt and the size of the machete in Gomez' hand, I decided to keep my mouth shut about Maria.

"I have business to do today. And I am shorthanded. You two will do this business for me. And in doing so, you will pay your debt to my family."

"Couldn't Tony just write a check?" Gomez hit me again. Then he put the machete back to my crotch.

"You will take the package in the Gremlin to the address we will give you. Once there, you will receive another package. Take that package to the second address you will be given and our business is concluded. If you refuse, I castrate you here in the desert."

"Well, I'm only 33, so I'm pretty sure I'm not done with my balls. I'll deliver the package."

"Yeah, I'm in," said Tony.

The goons began to untie us. When I was able to stand up, Gomez handed me a piece of paper. "The first address is where to deliver the package. The second is where to deliver the money."

"When we're done, what do we do with this piece of shit?" I pointed to the Gremlin.

"It's stolen, so do whatever you want with it."

"You stole that for us to deliver drugs in? Why couldn't you steal something fast like a Mustang or something reliable like a Honda?"

"Because when you steal a Mustang or a Honda, people want it back. Nobody wants a Gremlin back."

I looked at Tony. "He's got a point."

The brother looked me up and down. "Make certain you deliver the package and return all of the money to the second place. No stops, no talking with anyone, no calls. Get in the car and head straight to that address."

"What if the car dies before we get there?"

"It will run, at least through the end of the day. My men made sure of that."

"His men made sure of that," Tony repeated. "I feel so much better."

I leaned in towards Gomez and said, "You know, someday if we're brothers-in-law I hope you won't hold this against me."

"You marry my Maria?" More cursing in Spanish. People do that a lot down here. The cursing was followed by another punch in the kidneys. I buckled to my knees in pain at least three times on the way to the Gremlin.

"Hey Tony, how about you drive first?"

"Why not? At least until you stop spitting up blood."

***

If there is one thing worse than driving a 1974 Gremlin, it's driving one that hasn't been tuned up since 1974. A cloud of black smoke trailed behind us and the muffler must have had a hole in it. The car was loud, smoky, and slow. Its eight-track player had long since stopped working, a fact for which I was actually grateful because the only eight-tracks with us were by Conway Twitty. Somebody bought a shitty car and shitty music. They had then managed to let the shitty car get shittier over time so it would be just the right grade of shitty for the deep shit we found ourselves in today.

"You know this is a trap, don't you?" asked Tony.

"Yeah, I know that is BS about not having enough men today to do the job. He's sending us into something bad."

"When do you think it's going to go bad? When we drop off the drugs, or when we deliver the money?"

"I'm guessing it will be a little of both. I think he's sending us into a deal that he suspects will go bad. If it does, then he doesn't lose any of his own guys. We're in a stolen car and have just enough of a sordid past between us that the police won't think to tie it back to him. If the deal doesn't go bad, I'm guessing they're going to kill us anyway when we deliver the money."

"So, what are we going to do? Go to the police?"

"They are probably following us, so that won't work. I doubt we can pull up to a police station in a stolen car and cocaine or heroin, or whatever is in the backseat and be believable. Let's just keep driving and let me think."

It took a half hour of driving that old piece of junk to get to a major highway. From there, it was another 45 minutes back into Phoenix. When we pulled up at the drop site, I still didn't have a plan. So, I grabbed the bag and headed for the door. I knocked and a bald man, mid 40s, answered the door.

"Can I help you?"

"I have a delivery."

He looked at the Gremlin. Tony waved at him. "That's a pretty shitty delivery truck you have there."

I looked back towards the car. "You know, it kind of grows on you."

He didn't smile. "Who are you? I was expecting someone else."

I began to get very nervous. "We don't normally do this."

"Do what?"

"Deliver these kinds of packages."

"And what kind of package is it?"

At this point I was getting more anxious about the whole thing. I didn't want to play cat and mouse with this guy and I sure as heck didn't want to get shot. So, the part of me that didn't want to get shot was saying calm down, calm down. The part of me that was fed up was ready to punch the guy. The irritated part of me began to win out.

"Look do you have the money for the package or what?"

"Hey don't get snippy. I'm just being cautious because I wasn't expecting you to make the delivery. I wasn't expecting someone to be waiting outside in the car. And I sure as hell didn't expect that person to be waiting in a Gremlin. This is just a little odd for me, so excuse me for asking a few questions."

He slammed the door in a huff. Now what do I do? I turned back to the car and tried to mouth "now what" to Tony. He just kept saying, "Huh? I can't hear you."

The door opened again behind me and the bald man asked me to come inside. The living room was stark, with only a futon and a rickety coffee table that was covered in Chinese takeout containers. In the adjoining kitchen, I could see a variety of electronic devices, but had no idea what they were.

A tall man emerged from the kitchen, with long dark hair and a beard. He was dressed in a navy blue T-shirt, blue pants, and black boots. He looked military. I had a bad feeling.

"Do you have the drugs?"

"Yes, I think so."

"Great, you're under arrest."

***

Tony and I sat on the futon staring at the Chinese food containers. Although they seemed to be a few days old, they were making me hungry. I probably would have tried to rummage for something to sample if my hands weren't handcuffed behind me.

After waiting about 20 minutes for the DEA guys to finish their powwow in the kitchen, they came out to talk to us. "So, you guys are running drugs for Carlos Gomez?"

"Not exactly."

"We know they kidnapped you and we know they forced you to do this."

"You do?"

"Yes, we have an informant in his organization and Gomez is sort of on to us."

"He is?"

"Yes, but he thinks the informant is further down the food chain. He thought this was going to be a bust, and he was right about that."

"Then why send us in? We would have just told you he made us do it, a fact you seem to already know," I said.

The DEA agent responded, "Because the heroin package has a bomb in it?"

Tony shouted, "Son of a bitch. You can't trust anybody." Everybody looked at him. "What?"

"He believed the dealer who lived here was a snitch either way. So, the idea was if this was a bust, to blow up the dealer, the cops, and you. If it wasn't a bust, then just the dealer goes boom."

"See what I mean?" asked Tony. "Can't trust anybody."

I asked, "Then how did you know about the bomb? And why didn't we all go boom?"

"Like I said, we have a mole. And that mole is much higher up."

"So now what? Can we go home," I asked.

"No, you need to deliver that cash."

"But he's going to kill us when we do."

"We'll be watching. We have the location staked out. As soon as you hand over the money, we'll close in."

Tony asked, "Can we have guns?"

"No, you can't have guns."

"What about tasers?"

"Tony, you're not helping," I said. Turning back to the DEA agent, I asked, "What about my stuff?"

"Stuff?"

"Yeah, the framed jersey they stole from me at the hotel? How do I get it back?"

"If they still have it, it will probably be entered into evidence. You might not see it for a while, assuming they haven't unloaded it already."

"No, they still have it. They didn't even know what it was, so I doubt they found a buyer that fast. My guess is it's still in the van."

"You'll have to let us worry about that. Just give them the cash and we will be behind you."

"Yeah that's what I'm worried about. Who's going to be between me and his machete?"

***

Tony and I piled into the Gremlin one more time. I tossed the bag of cash in the backseat and Tony drove out of the neighborhood. It took twenty excruciatingly long minutes to get to the warehouse that was only a mile and a half away. Along the way, I pulled out my smartphone and opened the Uber app. I called for a car to meet me at the warehouse in thirty minutes. I put a special note in the request: "Shooting a movie at the location. Tell driver not to be alarmed by the sound of gunfire and/or explosions. None of it is real."

We arrived and two goons opened a large overhead door and we pulled inside. Four men with guns stood behind Carlos Gomez. Other workers were loading slender bags of what I can only assume were drugs into familiar looking wooden shapes. Once loaded, a worker with a key would close an inner door and lock it. Then he would close the glass frame that was attached to the hinge. They were then boxed and then loaded onto a pallet. That's why Byrne was moving thousands of jersey cases a week! They had a hidden compartment for shipping drugs. The DEA would never think to look into the world of sports memorabilia for a high volume drug dealer. Well, that is, until today.

Maybe that was what Eddie was trying to tell me in the picture! I'm such an idiot. Eddie must have allowed Byrne to use his frame as a model to build the prototype. While building it, they must have dismantled George's frame or damaged it. Byrne then gave Eddie the prototype as a replacement, and Eddie discovered the compartment. If somehow Eddie pieced together what Gomez and Byrne were really doing, he must have figured the only one who would believe him would be me. But if Eddie discovered the prototype, then had the fabric redone to conceal the hidden compartment, then...

Carlos greeted us with a grin. "Well done, well done. You have my money?"

"It's in the back." I opened the back door and reached for the bag. One of the goons pointed his gun at me.

"It's okay, I'm sure this man can be trusted," Carlos said, turning to me, "right, amigo?"

"Right," I answered. I held up the bag and walked slowly towards Carlos. I stopped just short of him and held it out with both hands. He looked inside, smiled and handed the bag to one of the goons.

"Well done, well done," he said. Then he pulled out a small caliber pistol from his jacket and shot me in the chest.

I could hear Tony screaming like a little girl. Shots started coming from everywhere as the DEA closed in. Tear gas canisters went off, followed by explosions. Carlos' gang had booby-trapped the warehouse. All hell was breaking loose.

Nobody paid attention to me because they all assumed I was dead. Only two people had been in the room when I was given the bulletproof vest at the dealer's house. And both of them were busy shooting at goons.

I surveyed my surroundings with one eye so as not to give away that I was still alive. Nobody was near. Chaos and smoke were my cover, so I stayed close to the ground and crawled to the van. Near the back door were a couple of dead goons. I pushed them out of the way and opened the back of the van. Just as I thought, the framed jersey was there. I grabbed it and crawled to a small door that was adjacent to the overhead door. I set the jersey down and looked outside. Two agents were covering the door for escaping goons.

"Sergeant Jones needs you both! Get in there."

"Our orders are to stay ..."

"The hell with your orders, your fellow officers are being slaughtered. Get in there!"

They ran past me into the fray, immediately getting disoriented by the tear gas. I stepped back in, grabbed the jersey and retreated outside. Just then, a black SUV pulled up and a driver got out.

"Help you with that, Sir?"

"No, just open the back, please."

Just then another explosion took out the third floor windows above us. Glass came crashing to the ground. The gunshots grew louder with the windows gone.

He opened the back hatch. "You say they're shooting a movie in there?"

"Yes, a Bruce Willis movie, I think."

"Sure seems real."

"You have no idea," I answered.

I jumped in the passenger seat and he started to write something on a clipboard. "You may want to hurry. In the next scene, the whole building comes down."

His eyes grew large. "Not on my new Escalade." The Uber driver threw the car in reverse, floored it for about 50 yards then hit the brake and spun the car around. Like that, we were off.

I asked, "You ever do any stunt driving?"

"No, why? You think I'm good enough for your movie?"

"I'll put in a good word with the director," I replied.

"Thanks!" He smiled and took me to my hotel.

Chapter Twenty

At this point, all I want to do is take a hot shower and go to bed. I've been kidnapped, beaten, arrested, shot in the chest, and inhaled a little teargas. So much for plans—Ramona wanted to know where I had been all day and why I had a hole in my shirt. I told her the entire story, start to finish. When I was done she stared at me for an awkward moment.

"Why is it always the bullshit? You are gone all day, probably with the whore with the legs, and you can only give me the bullshit."

"It's true! Look, look at this bullet hole." I showed her the hole in my shirt. Then I took it off to show her I still had on the bulletproof vest. "If I was lying, why would I be wearing this?"

"I'm sorry, my little baseball man." She hugged me and kissed my cheek. "Please forgive me for doubting you. Let me take you home and take care of you. My shift is almost over and I don't work tomorrow. You could check out of here and stay me with me all day tomorrow."

"You know, that sounds really amazing, but I think I'm just going to go up and grab a shower and go to bed early."

She looked at me suspiciously. "Okay, if you think that's best. But remember we have cameras." She pointed to the security camera at the reception desk. "If Ms. Leg Whore comes to see you, I will know about it."

"On my honor, the last thing I want tonight is any visitors. I'm going straight to bed."

"Okay, Mr. Baseball." She kissed me and stood up. Looking at the frame, she asked, "Do you want me to put this away?"

"No, I'll take it to my room." I kissed her goodnight and made for the elevator. As I rode up, I took in the jersey again. Why did Eddie switch frames? Why was this jersey so important to him? I wanted to look inside, but I was too exhausted. I never made it to the shower. I collapsed on the bed after taking off the vest and fell right to sleep. Tomorrow, I would check out before Ramona could call in to see if I had been a good boy the night before. I wondered if I would ever see her again.

***

The next morning, I checked out at 6:30. Next I went to a diner to have breakfast and read some baseball news. I had been in Phoenix for three weeks and hadn't paid a bit of attention to who had been traded, what rookies looked good, what veterans were on their last hope. Seemed like a shame to leave with another week of spring ball to go. But I had business to do and I really needed to get some distance between me and Ramona. I did notice that the day's top headline said that a drug kingpin had been shot and killed the day before and a local bat company owner was implicated in some related wrongdoing. I didn't read the story.

The coffee and the eggs got my brain moving. It was clear that Eddie had put the jersey into the prototype case before the auction. That means if he knew about the hidden passage, he might have known about the drugs. And maybe all this was Eddie's way of getting me to look into things—to somehow hope that I would see his clues and help expose Byrne and Gomez. Sort of a crazy-ass way of going about it, I decided. I thought about it a while longer. Then I smiled and paid my check. Eddie wasn't crazy at all.

***

Scottsdale was busy being a quiet suburb when I got there and that was fine with me. The last three weeks provided enough adventure for this trip and I was glad there were no bullets flying or things exploding. People were going about their days, completely unaware of me and the merchandise I was transporting. No suspicious cars were following me, not that I was checking every five seconds. You can't blame me for being a little paranoid, can you?

I arrived at Jessica's house to find Rainbow following her around the yard as she watered her flowers. By the look on her face, I could tell she needed rescuing from whatever long-winded story he was telling. Rainbow was there because I had asked him to meet us. My goal was to make sure the matter was settled with the Fungo Society. They needed to know that the case was closed and I needed to know they wouldn't be trying any more crazy stunts. Plus, they owed me money. And Rainbow had control of the checkbook.

Slowly, I got out of the car. My head still hurt and I was limping. But I was happy. Happy to be alive. Happy to know that Carlos was dead. Happy to have the package in my car. I opened the back of the SUV and slid the package out. It was a little awkward, especially since every inch of my body felt bruised from the day before, but I carried it myself across the lawn to the front door.

Rainbow patted me on the back. "That's my boy! I knew you would do it."

"Quick, I can't tell you how much this means to me," Jessica said. "How much do I owe you?"

"I think fifty thousand should cover it."

"Fifty thousand! How much did you pay for it?"

"I paid $1,500 for the Moonlight Graham jersey and traded it for this one."

Rainbow said, "Oh, he's just putting you on. How much do you want for it really, Quick?"

"Fifty thousand, Rainbow. Really." I answered.

His face turned red. "Why you greedy son of a bitch!"

"Mr. Quick! I thought we had a deal," Jessica responded.

"We did. For the Royals jersey. The fifty thousand is for the second jersey. And now I'm Mr. Quick? How can you be so cold after we…"

"That's quite enough," she cut me off, looking at Rainbow and back at me. "Wait. Did you say 'second jersey?' "

"This frame contains two jerseys. I'll give you the Royals jersey for the $1,500 we agreed plus expenses. But if you want the other jersey, you'll have to part with $50,000, which will be my commission when we sell it at auction"

"What are you talking about?"

I took the frame and laid it on the kitchen table. Carefully, I unlatched the case and opened the glass. Then, I pulled out white gloves, put them on and took gentle care in removing the Royals jersey from the case.

"Jessica, put a towel on the table so I can lay the jersey on it." After her help, I pulled out a knife and cut the light blue fabric along the edge of the frame.

"Quick, what the hell are you doing?" asked Rainbow.

Can you believe some people? Fussing over how the present is unwrapped instead of what's actually in the box?

"Eddie was trying to tell me something when he took the picture before killing himself." Jessica shuddered. "Sorry for that. He knew that if I saw that picture and went after his jersey, eventually I would figure it out. He was wearing two jerseys because he was trying to tell me that Byrne and Gomez were shipping drugs via a hidden compartment. But I also think he was trying to tell me a secret about this particular frame."

"And you think he hid another jersey under his Royals one," Jessica asked.

"Eddie kept a secret from you and your mother all these years. The Royals jersey wasn't what he wanted back. It's what's under the Royals jersey."

"Why risk taking this to auction if something that valuable was underneath," asked Rainbow.

"My guess is he felt it was safe hidden inside the frame. It was the one asset he hadn't listed in his will or insurance and he had a receipt saying he sold it years ago. That makes it a little tricky to outright gift it to an heir. There would be taxes and his creditors would want most of the value from it. This way Jessica would own the Royals jersey and the contents of the frame and have an auction receipt to prove it. Once the dust settles on his financial troubles, she gifts it back to him or just sells it and uses the money to take care of her parents. He didn't count on Byrne, or anyone for that matter, bidding against Jessica for the jersey."

I kept cutting. Feeling along the fabric, I looked for any hint of a hinge or a keyhole. Feeling nothing, I continued cutting down the left side and across the bottom. As the knife slid into the corner, we all heard the sound of metal on metal. Then I pulled back the fabric to reveal a small keyhole, flush with the wood.

"Do you have the key," Jessica asked.

"No, but I brought a few tools with me that come in handy in these situations," I answered. That elicited a look of disdain from Jessica and a chuckle from Rainbow. It's not like I'm a jewel thief, for heaven's sake! But sometimes when you come across granny's tobacco cards in a locked shadowbox at auction, one needs to verify their authenticity, right?

I slid an appropriately sized metal file into the keyhole. It didn't work. I reached for a smaller one and tried it again. No luck. I was just about to curse aloud when I remembered a lock George once opened for me. This was based on one of his frames; maybe the lock was similar too. That particular box contained a baseball signed by the 1875 Cincinnati Reds. My knees buckled when he opened it.

I took my two smallest files and inserted them into the lock. Then I pressed each in opposing directions. The lock turned and two bulges popped up in the fabric that was still attached. I cut the rest of the fabric away and Rainbow and Jessica could see two hinges that had emerged from the wooden frame. The craftsmanship was amazing. The keyhole and hinges were flush with the wood when locked. The latch system was designed to lift the hinges up from the wood so the hidden compartment could be opened, yet be completely undetectable when the latch was closed and the fabric was over it.

I gently opened the wooden door that was on back of the frame. The space was tight, only an inch deep. A layer of wax paper hid the treasure below. Then I pulled it away, causing Jessica to gasp.

Rainbow mumbled, "Holy shit!"

Then he yelled "Holy shit!"

In the hidden panel sat a wool baseball jersey, white home flannel. Carefully, I took the edge and inched it out of the compartment. Brooklyn was embroidered across the front in faded Dodger blue. The three of us stared silently.

"It is real," whispered Rainbow.

"Yes, it's authentic."

"Is it the one?" Jessica was still staring.

"If there is a number 35 on the back, it's real. Several years ago, a collector paid a lot of money for a fake. I spotted it immediately because it had the number 3 on the back. Of course everyone knows that Ruth wore number 3 on the Yankees, and that's where the forger went wrong. There was a player on the Dodgers who was wearing 3, so Ruth wore 35 that year."

I gently picked up the jersey and held it up for Jessica and Rainbow. She gulped and began to cry. Rainbow could only repeat, "Holy shit."

I turned the jersey around and took it all in. This is art to me. You can have your Picassos and Van Goghs. Give me an authentic piece of baseball history and I'm in awe. Inside the collar, the Babe's name was embroidered just below was the A.G. Spalding Bros. tag. Attached to it was a size 46 flag tag. Looking down the back, this jersey had something that made it unique among jerseys of its day. The fabric was longer than normal and had an extra gusset with a drawstring so the Babe could tie it to his pants. This kept his belly from untucking his jersey.

It was in beautiful condition. And it was right in my grasp. I suppose I could have taken it out before I came, replaced the fabric and simply returned the Royals jersey to Jessica. But there was the matter of her mother to consider. Some lucky bastard with considerably more gelt than I have would own this soon enough. But for a few more moments, I enjoyed its company.

"This will pay for your mother's expenses and keep her in the nicer home. Can you stall them for another month? I think we can get more if I have a few weeks to find the right auction."

"Yes, I can cover it for one more month."

Rainbow gave me a pat on the back. "Well done, my boy. Well done."

"I can't thank you enough, Quick." Jessica gave me a hug. I was hoping for much more, given my bravery and all the risks I took to deliver this treasure. However, with Rainbow in the room, it must have felt like her dad was watching. I had to settle for a peck on the cheek.

"Well, I have to be going. Flight to catch. Rainbow, do you have something for me?"

He handed me an envelope and looked around. "No word on where this came from."

I opened it and pulled out a check. I looked at Rainbow, puzzled by the cloak and dagger routine. "Rainbow, this check says it's from the Fungo Society."

He hushed me. "And nobody needs to know that." He looked both ways again.

"Not even her," I asked? Jessica smiled at both of us.

He pondered for a moment then shook his head. God love him, Rainbow is a strange man. "Perhaps you will work for us again," he said. "There are a lot of us." Then he leaned in and whispered, "More of us than you'd imagine."

***

I stepped out of the warm air of baggage claim and into the cold reality of March in Indiana. I was back in my home city. Indianapolis always seems to get one more blast of wintry weather before the end of March. We expect it as much as we expect to watch the college basketball tournament while we're holed up and bitterly awaiting spring. Piles of dirty snow lined either side of the road on the way home from the airport.

When I arrived at my place, I was greeted with a pungent aroma coming from the kitchen. Milk left on the counter at room temperature for three weeks becomes a solid that fills your home with a demonic revenge funk. Milk must be drunk, not ignored. If it is ignored, it becomes vile. That goes for girlfriends, too, but that's another story.

I tossed the milk, sprayed some air freshener and found that the two smells combined was even worse. I retreated to the bedroom and realized I hadn't checked my messages since I had turned my phone back on after the flight.

After a couple of can you find this jersey or that artifact type messages, I played one that almost made me fall out of bed. "Quick, it's Ted Arnett at the Baseball Hall of Fame. It seems we have a problem with the Ted Williams contract your uncle donated to the museum. It's a forgery. Please call us at once."

Upcoming Quick Mysteries:

72 Hours in Savannah
Tangled in The Web
Yankee Doodle Dead
Crime of the Ancient Mariner

ABOUT THE AUTHOR

Jeff Stanger writes funny novels that usually have the game of baseball as a backdrop. You don't have to be a student of the game or even a fan to enjoy them, however. There is enough mystery, danger, and even romance to keep you on the edge of your seat. His current work includes the Quick Baseball Mystery Series, which follows the exploits of a rare baseball memorabilia dealer who always seems to land himself in the middle of a criminal case to be solved. In addition, Stanger has written *Trolley Dodgers* which follows the Midwest college town of Bloomington, IN as they try to buy the Los Angeles Dodgers. He also wrote *Kansaska*, a funny look back at the semi-pro minor leagues of the 1940's.

Stanger lives and writes in Indianapolis, Indiana. Along with writing, he is a member of the faculty at The Fund Raising School at the Lilly Family School of Philanthropy at Indiana University and a nonprofit consultant.

Other books by this author:
Trolley Dodgers
Kansaska
Facts Cause Cancer